A Horse Called Willing

Rebecca Martin

Christian Light Publications, Inc.
Harrisonburg, Virginia

Christian Light Publications, Inc., Harrisonburg, Virginia 22801
© 1998 by Christian Light Publications, Inc.
All rights reserved. Published 1998
Printed in the United States of America

3rd printing, 2008

Cover by Michelle Beidler

ISBN 978-0-87813-576-9

Publisher's Note

A Horse Called Willing is set among people who have chosen a life uncluttered by today's technology and conveniences. While culture sometimes replaces spirituality, it doesn't in this book. This warmhearted story portrays important lessons that apply to all of us.

Contents

1. Race in the Pasture

The wind whistled past Joel's ears as he ran, pumping his legs harder and harder. His elbows worked like pistons. His breath came in gasps. His heart seemed almost to burst from his chest.

But it was no use. Lady and Jim were far ahead of Joel, and they knew it. Down the pasture raced Lady, her mane and tail streaming in the wind, her hooves pounding. Beside her ran Jim, as only a dog can run, his legs first splayed out front and back, and then doubled beneath him.

Joel fell into a panting heap on the grass. Seconds later, his brother Elam landed almost on top of him. They rolled on the soft grass, laughing in sheer joy. "I guess we'll never win a race with Lady and Jim," gasped ten-year-old Joel.

"No, but I couldn't care less. It's the race—not the winning—that's fun," Elam replied wisely. He was two years older.

Joel sat up and gazed down the pasture towards the creek. The horse and the dog were still going flat-out, each trying to win. Joel laughed, "Lady and Jim take the race seriously."

Elam sat up too. "How can they expect to stop before they get to the creek?" he cried.

At that moment, Lady lurched back on her haunches, coming to an abrupt halt. The dog didn't bother to stop, but bounded into the creek, throwing

1

up a geyser of water, thoroughly soaking his good friend Lady.

Elam hooted, "I guess Jim figures he won the race because he went farther than Lady."

Joel was shaking with laughter. "See, now he doused Lady again when he shook himself. Lady must be insulted. Watch her toss her head!"

"They're coming back our way now," Elam said. Once again there was the muted thunder of hooves as Lady flew towards them over the turf. Soon she and the dog slowed to a walk. Jim romped up to Elam, wagging his tail. His golden coat was still soggy. The pleased look on his sharp collie face seemed to say, "Did you see that? I won the race with Lady."

Lady lowered her head and sniffed at Joel's shirt. A slim brown horse with graceful limbs, she was a lady indeed.

"Hey, you're tickling me," chuckled Joel, wriggling away from Lady's muzzle. "What do you want me to do, race you again? I'm tuckered out. You and Jim will have to race without Elam and me."

Lady seemed to understand. She tossed her head and stamped her hooves in a challenge to Jim. Then she was off across the pasture again with the dog in hot pursuit.

"It's harder going uphill," observed Elam as he watched the pair heading up towards the barn.

Joel squinted against the evening sun. "Lady is definitely winning this time. See? She reached the gate before Jim."

Elam nodded. He was pulling out his watch. "I guess it's time we were going up to the house. Mom will have supper ready."

2

The two boys trudged side by side up the hill. The evening was quiet except for birdsongs and the clink of harness from the field beside them.

"Harvey is still cultivating his corn in our field," Joel remarked. His eyes followed the team of heavy work horses as they plodded between the rows of waving corn.

"I guess it's just as much Harvey's land as ours, since he's renting it," Elam corrected him.

Joel felt slightly irked. Sometimes it seemed to him that Elam's chief pleasure in life was correcting him. He persisted, "But the land is still ours. And maybe one day it will be yours—or mine."

"Okay, okay. It'll probably be mine. At least Mom keeps talking about how it will be once I'm big enough to run the farm," Elam replied.

Joel nodded. "But that's still a long way off."

"Yes. So in the meantime, we'll keep on gardening!" Elam motioned towards the acre of land Mom had kept after Dad died.

Joel sighed as he looked at the rows and rows of strawberries, tomatoes, and other vegetables. "We'll probably spend most of the summer bent double in the garden," he said glumly.

Elam looked at him sharply. "What's so bad about that? We need something to do, don't we?"

"Yes, but I'd rather be driving a team for haying, like Harvey's boys," Joel replied.

Elam said nothing more. He bounded up the porch steps calling, "Supper ready, Mom?"

"You're right on time," beamed Mom as she placed a bowl of potatoes on the table. She watched fondly as her two golden-haired boys hurried to wash up at the sink. Mom's own hair had once been golden. But now, though she was only thirty-five, there were streaks of gray.

After prayer, they began eating in silence. Often the boys chattered during mealtime; but tonight, Joel was busy thinking. He pictured how it probably looked over in neighbor Harvey's kitchen at this moment. The ten children would be gathered around the table with their mother and father. After supper the boys would help do chores in the barn— in two barns, actually, because they kept some livestock in Mom's barn too.

How would it be, Joel mused, *to have both a mother and a father?* He had been only a year old when his father, Lester Stutzman, died. "How long," he asked, suddenly breaking the silence, "was Dad sick before he died?"

Mom looked startled. She had been thinking about Dad too. "Three years," she answered softly. "Elam was just a baby when we discovered Dad had cancer."

"He took treatments too, didn't he?" asked Elam. They had discussed most of these questions before, but every now and then it felt good to talk about Dad again.

"Yes, he had radiation treatments. For awhile we thought he was better. Then when Joel was six months old Dad became very sick again," Mom replied.

"Did he have a lot of pain?" Joel couldn't remember asking this before. He wouldn't have thought to ask it either, except last Sunday they had visited an elderly grandmother with cancer. Mom had said she was taking medication for pain.

Mom's eyes were moist as she turned to look at

him. "Joel, your dad always said the pain wasn't too bad, that he could endure it without medication. But I think—in fact, I know—the pain was often worse than he admitted."

"How did you know?" wondered Joel.

Mom stared unseeingly out the window. "Dad spent many hours reading. Often he read the Bible. Sometimes he read the *Martyrs Mirror,* you know, the big book that tells of our Christian forefathers who were tortured and killed for their faith. Once Dad said to me, 'I haven't suffered anything like those early Christians suffered.'"

Mom turned again to Joel. "That told me a lot about Dad's suffering."

Joel nodded. Silence descended on the kitchen again, broken only by the ticking of the clock. Even though he didn't remember his dad, Joel had a warm feeling inside as he thought of him now—Dad had faith in God . . . in spite of the pain.

2. Pat, the Pig

"Well, I guess it's chore-time," Elam said in a grownup kind of voice as he pushed his chair away from the table. "You coming, Joel?"

Joel shrugged. "Might as well, though there are hardly enough chores for two people, with only Porker and the cats to feed."

Elam made no reply. He slipped into his boots and strode purposefully out through the washhouse and down the porch steps.

Joel hurried after him. "Sometimes I wish Harvey Yoders had mostly girls instead of mostly boys."

Elam stopped in mid-stride and gave him a quizzical stare. "You have the oddest wishes."

"I mean," Joel explained quickly, "if they didn't have so many boys, Harveys would need us to help with chores. Maybe they'd let us feed the livestock they keep in our barn. But with four boys out of school, they simply don't need us."

"I see," said Elam. "Well, we can't change that. At least we can feed Porker." He opened a barn door and went to a pen. Their half-grown pig was black and white, with one black ear and one white. Porker came grunting happily towards them. "Feed me, I'm hungry," he seemed to say.

Elam gave Porker an affectionate slap. "You can't really be hungry. Why, you do nothing but eat all day!"

"He'll be more than fat by butchering time," Joel commented.

Suddenly a loud shrieking began at the far end of the barn. Joel jumped, then smiled sheepishly. "What a racket those sows make when they see someone coming to feed them!" he exclaimed. Twelve hungry sows joined together in one ear-splitting roar.

Elam hurried to feed Porker. "Let's go see which of Harvey's boys came over to do chores tonight." Together they dashed to the other end of the barn. There was nineteen-year-old Paul, the oldest Yoder son, slopping feed into the sows' troughs. Soon the only noise was the slurping sounds made as the sows gulped their supper.

Paul paused near one of the sow's pens, and Joel went over to join him. "This one has ten piglets," Paul told him. "Well, I guess there are eleven, but that runt won't make it." He hung one leg over the partition and nudged the runt with the toe of his boot. The poor, thin piglet tried feebly to run away. Its legs were barely able to carry it.

Joel's heart went out to the little creature. "What's the matter with it?"

Paul shrugged. "Not getting enough to eat, I guess. It's not strong enough, and the others bully it away from the sow."

"I should bottle-feed it!" Joel exclaimed impulsively.

Paul's black eyebrows shot up until they nearly touched his black hair. "Well, I never!" he said.

"Wouldn't it work?" Joel asked.

Paul looked down at Joel's pleading blue eyes. Like the rest of the Yoder family, he was fond of

7

Mary Stutzman's boys and couldn't bear to see them sad. Even though Paul felt it would be useless to bottle-feed a pig, he said, "You can try it if you like."

Joel scooped up the piglet. He turned and saw Elam staring at him. Anxiously he scanned his older brother's face. He knew he would need Elam to help him with such a project.

"We better take it indoors. The poor thing is shivering," said Elam.

Joel grinned widely. Elam would help him!

But as Joel hurried with the piglet towards the house, more misgivings came to his mind. "Will Mom mind having a pig in the house?" he worried.

"We'll see," was Elam's response.

The piglet struggled feebly against Joel's shirtfront as they entered the kitchen. "Mom, do you have a fire going in the woodstove?" Joel asked.

Mom turned. Her eyebrows rose too, but not as far as Paul's had. "Yes, I do. What have you there? A sick piggy? We should get a cardboard box for it and put it right here on the open oven door."

"Good idea," said Joel gratefully. Mom's response surprised him. She knew just what to do!

Mom sensed his surprise. "Your dad used to do that sometimes," she explained. "On cold winter nights, he'd bring in the littlest piggies to keep them warm." Then she added in a businesslike way, "We should have some clean straw for this box."

Joel thrust the piglet into Elam's hands. "Hold it. I'll get the straw." As he dashed to the barn, he thought about what Mom had said. So Dad used to bring piggies inside too! Joel felt the warmth inside again. No matter that Paul Yoder didn't think it would work to bottle-feed a piglet. If Dad were here,

8

he would approve.

Soon they had prepared a cozy nest of straw for the piglet. But it refused to settle down. With pitiful little "oinks," it staggered around in the box.

"It's hungry," declared Mom. She bustled into the pantry and returned with an old baby bottle. Joel watched as she warmed some milk and filled the bottle. Then she reached under the piglet and cradled it with one hand while holding the bottle with the other.

"Look at it!" crowed Joel gleefully. The piglet slurped hungrily at the rubber nipple.

Mom smiled. "You boys should think of a name for this pig, instead of just saying 'it.' "

Joel looked at Elam. "How about 'Runt'?" Elam suggested.

Joel shook his head. "This pig won't be a runt for very long. How about Pat?"

Elam nodded. "Pat, the Pig. That's a nice short name."

By bedtime Pat had downed two bottles of milk. "It's a good thing we can get all the skim milk we need from Harveys," Mom said. "We're going to need a lot for this little piggy!"

When Joel went up to bed, Pat lay sound asleep in the straw. But several hours later, Joel was awakened by a strange sound. It took him a moment to realize what he heard. Pat was squealing, down in the kitchen!

Joel shone his flashlight at the alarm clock. Almost midnight. "Hungry again," he groaned as he got out of bed. By the time he had pulled on his trousers and started downstairs, however, the squealing had stopped.

9

Curious, Joel went to check on his new charge. A lamp was burning, and there was Mom, feeding Pat!

"Oh, Mom, I didn't know we'd have to do this at night too," he said apologetically.

Mom smiled. "I figured it would happen, and kept some milk warm on the back of the stove."

"Will Pat wake up again before morning? I could do the next feeding," Joel offered.

"Oh, I don't mind," Mom replied.

"Well, thanks," Joel said with feeling. He trudged back upstairs and crawled under the covers. Before drifting off to sleep, he whispered, "Thank You, God, for a mom like that."

3. Willingness

"Can you boys guess what you will have to do as soon as we're finished eating?" Mom asked at breakfast the next morning.

It didn't take Joel long to figure it out. "Fetch milk at Harveys!"

"Right. Pat has drunk the last drop. She's sleeping right now, but it won't be long till she wakes again," Mom predicted.

After devotions Joel grabbed the milk pail and headed for the door. Then he stopped. "Shouldn't we take a bigger pail?"

"Maybe we should," Mom agreed. "Here's one."

Soon Joel and Elam were knocking at Harveys' back door. Lizzie, the oldest of their three girls, met them. Lizzie was eleven and, like Paul, she had thick black hair and dark brown eyes. "My, you brought a big pail!" she exclaimed.

"Well, you see, we're bottle-feeding a baby pig. And she's a real pig—eating all the time," Joel exclaimed.

"Bottle-feeding a pig!" squealed Lizzie. She almost spilled the milk as she poured it into their pail. "I'd like to see that."

"You may if you like," Joel said with a shrug. He was often sorry none of Harvey's seven boys were close to his own age. The three girls were eleven, ten, and eight—all in a row.

11

"We're going to be busy cultivating garden today though," Elam put in.

"Oh," said Lizzie. "No time for visitors. Well, maybe tomorrow? We could bring the milk for you."

"Yes, you better come tomorrow if you want to see Pat being bottle-fed. Mom thinks she'll be drinking from a bowl soon," Joel told her as he turned to go.

As they neared home, Elam said, "We'd better hurry. I think I hear Pat squealing now!"

Joel cocked his head. "You're right!" His stride quickened.

"Just in time," Mom said, taking the milk. "Will you get Lady while I feed Pat? I'll be out soon."

Joel watched her for a moment, then hurried after Elam. He climbed onto the pasture gate and shouted at the top of his voice, "Lady! Here, Lady! Gee-up. Cultivating time." Then he turned to Elam with a frown. "The wind must be the wrong way, or something. She doesn't seem to hear me. She didn't even lift her head when I called."

"No wonder. She's way down by the creek," Elam pointed out. "I'll go and get her."

Just then something shot past them like a streak of lightning. It was Jim, heading down the hill towards Lady.

"Jim heard you say 'Go and get her,'" laughed Joel. "Do you think Lady will come?"

Elam vaulted over the gate and started after the dog. "I don't know, but I'm going too, just to make sure. It's time we got started with the cultivating."

Joel stayed at the top of the hill to watch. He was in no big hurry to start cultivating the garden anyway. He chuckled as Jim ran up to Lady and bounded around her, barking insistently. From the way Lady swung her head, Joel guessed she was snorting at the dog. She didn't appreciate being barked at.

Suddenly her head went up. She had seen Elam. Obediently she trotted up to him and let him grab her halter. Elam broke into a run to keep up with her. "Open the gate, Joel!" he called.

Joel unfastened the padlock. After the pair had hurried through, he closed the gate and followed them. By the time he reached the garden, Elam had harnessed Lady and was hitching her to the cultivator.

The cultivator was a very light implement with one large wheel, several tines for cultivating, and two handles for guiding. Even for a small horse like Lady, it was easy to pull.

"Come on, Joel. Let's go!" Elam cried impatiently. He had taken his place at the back of the cultivator, grasping the handles.

Joel dragged his feet as he approached Lady's head. "I'm tired of this job," he muttered. "We went through the whole garden last week—up and down, up and down, between the rows. Now we have to do the whole thing again."

"I don't know what you're grumbling about, but please hurry!" Elam urged.

"Okay, okay," Joel said, still mumbling. He grasped Lady's halter. His job was to lead her while Elam made sure the tines of the cultivator stayed well down in the soil.

"Giddap!" called Elam. Lady strained into the harness. The soil began crumbling away from the tines. Plod, plod, plod, went Lady's hoofs. Down between two rows of tomatoes they went, then up

13

again, between two more rows of tomatoes, then down between two rows of beans . . . to Joel the morning stretched endlessly before him.

Mom came out, carrying a hoe. "I gave Pat an extra bottle of milk so she'll be happy for awhile," she reported. She began to swing her hoe methodically.

Joel's right arm ached from pulling at Lady's halter. He tried the left arm. Soon it ached too. "When can we stop for a rest?" he asked irritably.

Elam was surprised. "Stop for a rest? We've barely begun."

"Well, I'm tired already," Joel growled.

He hadn't meant for Mom to hear him, but she had. "Do you know a good remedy for tiredness?" she asked.

"Rest, I s'pose," Joel replied shortly.

Mom nodded. "Of course. But there's another remedy that helps even if we keep going. The secret is in one word. Can you guess what the word is?"

Joel thought for a moment. "Lemonade?" he asked hopefully.

Behind him, Elam burst out laughing. He could see Mom was pinching back a smile too. Joel scowled. He didn't like having people laughing at him.

"Lemonade is a good idea too," Mom assured him. "Even a drink of cold water would do. But the word I had in mind starts with a 'w.' It is the word *willing*. If we work willingly, we don't feel as tired as if we work grudgingly."

"I see," said Joel. He didn't feel very willing.

Finally, Elam agreed to stop. "Lady needs a rest," he said as they paused under the big tree at the far

14

end of the garden.

Joel looked at Lady's heaving sides. "You think only of her, never about how tired I am," he grumbled.

Elam looked at him with a smile that irked Joel even more. "Have you forgotten what Mom said? We only have to be willing, then we don't grow tired."

"That's not what she said!" Joel objected hotly. "She only said it helps to be willing."

Elam shrugged. "The same thing."

Joel disagreed, but decided not to say anything more. He felt too tired to quarrel.

All too soon, Elam urged Lady and Joel on again. Every now and then, Joel thought of Mom's words. He knew she was right. But how was he supposed to be willing when he really didn't feel willing?

After awhile an unmistakable sound drifted to them from the porch. "Pat's squealing!" yelled Joel. "Can I feed the pig, and you lead Lady, Mom?"

"All right," said Mom, dropping her hoe to take Lady's halter.

Joel started off at a run across the garden. Behind him he heard Elam say, "He doesn't look very tired now."

Sheepishly, Joel slowed to a walk. It was true, he had forgotten his weariness at the thought of feeding Pat.

He picked up the pig from its box on the sunny porch. "Feeding you doesn't make me tired," Joel mused to the pig. "It must be because I'm willing to feed you. I guess I should learn to work willingly in the garden too, the way Elam does."

Pat merely grunted in reply.

4. Lady's Accident

"No cultivating today!" Joel called happily as he ran through the pasture to Lady. "Shall we have a race?"

Lady pricked up her ears. She knew what Joel wanted! Immediately she began pawing the ground as though to ask, "When do we start?"

Joel didn't bother with a starting signal. He simply took off down the hill. Lady would win anyway, even if he had a head start.

But for once, Lady did not win. Something horrible happened instead. She had galloped past Joel when suddenly she went down in a sprawling heap with a shrieking whinny.

Joel ran to her. "Lady! What's the matter?" he gasped. She lay with her head down and her legs crumpled beneath her. Joel felt sick. Lady's breath came out like a moan.

Joel saw a hole in the ground near Lady's front feet. It was a groundhog burrow by the looks of it. "She must have stepped into that hole and hurt her leg!" Joel told himself. "I must run for help." He turned to go, then stopped again. What if Lady tried to struggle to her feet? That would be the worst thing she could do—especially if the leg was broken.

"Oh, Lady," cried Joel. "What shall I do? I should stay here, but we need help!"

Lady stopped moaning and looked at him. She

16

couldn't answer his question.

Suddenly Joel heard a shout from further down the pasture. There, coming toward him along the creek bank, were the three Yoder girls. Sometimes they took that route just for fun when coming to the Stutzmans.

"We came to see Pat!" Lizzie called before they were near.

"Hurry up! Lady's hurt, and I can't leave her," Joel shouted. Never before in his life had he been so glad to see Lizzie and Dorcas and Ruth.

Lizzie's eyes were wide. "What's wrong?"

"Lady's hurt badly. Can you go up and tell Mom or Elam to call the vet? I have to stay with Lady."

Without another word, the three girls were off. Joel watched them gratefully. Sometimes it seemed to him that girls were giggly creatures who couldn't take very much. But it looked as if you could depend on them in a real emergency.

Joel could see the house from where he sat. Moments after the girls reached the porch, he saw Elam sprinting down the road toward the pay-phone booth. Mom came hurrying to the pasture. Breathing hard, she sank to her knees beside Lady. "Poor girl—poor girl," she soothed as she stroked the horse's head.

"Do you think her leg's broken?" Joel asked anxiously.

Mom touched the right foreleg. Lady flinched. "It must be this one," she said. "It doesn't look crooked."

"Could a horse's broken leg heal?" was Joel's next question.

Mom face was somber. "I don't know. Sometimes

17

horses with broken legs have to be put down."

"Put down?" Joel wasn't sure at first what she meant. Then he realized the meaning of the words and cried, "Oh, no!"

Mom didn't say anything. Her head was bent down, and he couldn't see her face. He knew how much Mom liked Lady. More than once she had said, "Lady is the perfect horse for a woman to drive."

Lizzie, Dorcas, and Ruth came huffing and puffing down the hill again. They were full of questions. Joel wished they would be quiet, but Mom was very patient with them.

It seemed like ages until the vet came. Finally his four-wheel-drive truck came in the lane. Elam opened the pasture gate, and the vet drove right into the field. He was careful not to drive too near Lady though, for fear of disturbing her.

Mr. Duval was short and stocky. "Hi," he said briefly to no one in particular. He stooped and ran a practiced hand over Lady's leg. Joel could see fear in Lady's eyes, but she lay quietly while this stranger examined her.

Mr. Duval straightened his back. "Not broken. A bad sprain."

Although Joel didn't usually speak easily to strangers, he couldn't help asking, "Can it heal?"

A smile crinkled Mr. Duval's eyes as he looked into Joel's anxious face. "It certainly can, if you take good care of her. But she will have to stay in her stall for weeks. And it may be a couple of months before you can use her on the road."

Joel looked at Mom. He was thinking, *Months! But how will we get to church and to town? Who will cultivate our garden?*

Mom's thoughts were not for herself, however. She asked, "How will we get Lady to the barn?"

"You keep her quiet, and I'll put the leg into a splint," said Mr. Duval. Joel watched in fascination as the vet produced the necessary materials from his big bag. Soon Lady's leg was bound up in a very sturdy-looking splint!

"Now, if she'd rather, she can just lie here for a bit. But stay with her," Mr. Duval instructed. "Once she gets up—as I'm sure she will—lead her to the barn." He looked at Elam and Joel, then back at Mom. "It might be a good idea to have a grown man here. To help control her if she—"

Elam interrupted, "Lady is a quiet horse."

"But you can't predict what she'll do if she's in pain. And she'll have quite a bit when she tries to put any weight on that leg. I expect she will learn very quickly to put most of her weight on the other three legs. Still," Mr. Duval repeated, "if you can, get a man to help."

Mom looked at the Yoder girls. "Maybe one of Harvey's boys?"

The Yoder girls looked at one another. "Dad and Paul are away," Dorcas said frowning.

Lizzie declared firmly, "Vernon could come. Let's go get him." And they were off across the pasture. The vet walked to his truck, waved, and drove away.

Joel's eyes followed the girls. "They talk too much," he said to Mom.

Mom chuckled. "They're nice little girls. They came to watch us feeding Pat, you know, and they never complained about missing out on that."

"I really don't think they talk much more than you do," Elam said. Joel was squatted near Lady's

19

head, stroking her mane.

"Humph!" snorted Joel. "You can—"

"Boys, boys," came Mom's steady voice. To get their mind off their quarrel, she added quickly, "Do you think Vernon will be here soon?"

Elam shrugged. "I don't think we need him. Why didn't the vet think I could handle Lady?" After all, Vernon was only four years older than he.

Lady seemed to agree with Elam. She raised her head, gave a pained whinny, and struggled to her feet.

"Atta girl," said Elam. "Here goes, up to the barn. Careful on your leg."

Joel noticed a funny expression on Mom's face that was part frown and part smile.

Lady quickly caught on how to take it easy. She hobbled along, scarcely putting any weight on her right foreleg.

The four of them had just reached the pasture gate when Vernon arrived. He said, "Shall I take her? The girls said you need a man to lead Lady to the barn." Even though he was sixteen, Vernon was only a fraction of an inch taller than Elam.

Elam eyed the neighbor boy. "We're managing all right," he said evenly.

Vernon folded his arms across his chest. "Then why did you send for me?"

"We didn't. The vet did. He doesn't realize how well we know this horse." Elam led Lady through the barn door and to her stall.

Joel felt uncomfortable because Vernon was plainly aggravated. Elam had been rude, yet Joel understood why he acted the way he did. Having a stranger lead Lady made no sense at all!

"I'm sorry you came over for nothing," Mom apologized to Vernon. "I guess the vet thought Lady would be difficult to handle or something."

A smile replaced the stubborn look on Vernon's face. "That's all right. I'm glad she wasn't a problem. And I hope she gets well soon." He turned to leave.

5. Accepting Help

The weather turned very warm on the day of Lady's accident. Joel and Elam were supposed to mow the lawn that afternoon. They took turns pushing the old reel mower. "Whew, it's hot!" exclaimed Joel when it was his turn. "This is hard work, and I'm so tired."

Elam grinned. "Maybe you should take some of Mom's 'Be willing' remedy."

Joel scowled. "I wonder how many times you've reminded me of that since yesterday morning."

"Once or twice," Elam said carelessly. "Come on, take your turn around the lawn."

Joel was still scowling as he pushed off. Before he was halfway around the lawn, he stopped and said excitedly, "Harvey Yoders are coming in the lane. What could they want in the middle of the day like this?"

"I don't know, but why don't you keep on mowing?" Elam asked crossly.

"I'm going inside. I want to hear what Harveys and Mom talk about," Joel declared.

"Okay, okay," Elam grumbled. He wanted to go indoors too.

But instead of going into the house, Mom walked with Harvey and Elsie to the barn. "Of course. They came to see about Lady," whispered Joel as he followed them.

Harvey Yoder was tall. His black hair and beard were streaked with gray. Elsie was tall too—maybe four inches taller than Mom. Her eyes were gray, matching her once-brown hair.

Harvey walked into Lady's stall and examined her leg. "A good sturdy splint," he commented. "But it'll take a while until she's roadworthy again."

"Yes. I wanted to talk to you about that," said Mom.

"We figured," Elsie replied with a smile. "That's why we came. Would you like to have the neighbors take you along on Sundays?"

Mom hesitated. "Most of the neighbors have big families and their surreys are full. If someone had a horse I could borrow for awhile. . . ."

Harvey's brow was wrinkled. "We thought of that. I wish we had a spare. But with all our boys . . ." He gestured with his hands. "Nor can I think of anyone in the neighborhood who might have an extra horse."

"What about Leyland?" Mom asked.

Bob Leyland was a horse dealer. Whenever someone needed a horse, he could talk to Bob, and Bob would come up with something.

"You mean you'd want to buy a second horse?" Harvey questioned.

"Not really." Mom had it all thought out. "We hope Lady will recover. But Bob has so many horses around his place. I've heard he sometimes boards them at other farms. If he should happen to have a quiet horse we could board for awhile—and use, of course . . ." Her voice trailed off as she waited expectantly.

Harvey nodded. "Not a bad idea. Shall I ask Leyland?"

"I would appreciate that," Mom said sincerely.

"We'll be off then," Harvey said, turning to his wife.

Joel and Elam stood with Mom on the porch and watched their neighbors drive away. "I don't know what we'd do without Harvey and Elsie," Mom said softly.

"When Lady was hurt this morning, Lizzie had said her dad was away," Elam recalled. "Harvey must have come over as soon as he got home."

Mom gave Elam a meaningful look. "You understand, don't you? How grateful we should be for their help? *All* their help?"

Joel could see Elam was squirming, and he knew why. Mom was reminding him of the ungrateful way he had acted when Vernon offered to help.

Elam looked down at his bare feet. "Yes, Mom."

"It isn't always easy," Mom admitted. "I had a lot of learning to do too, after Dad died, about accepting people's help, I mean."

There was a flicker of surprise in Elam's face. It had never occurred to him that Mom found it hard to accept help too.

Then Mom laid a hand on Elam's shoulder. "At the same time, it makes me happy you boys can take care of more and more jobs around here. That means we won't have to depend on others as much as time goes on."

Neither of the boys knew what to say. After a moment Elam cleared his throat and said, "We'd better get at that lawn-mowing again, Joel."

"Yes, we'd better," Joel agreed willingly. Heading across the lawn to the mower, they did not see the tears Mom brushed from her eyes.

24

Both boys worked with a will after that. Joel no longer thought about being tired. When the yard was done, Mom came out on the porch with some cookies and cold lemonade. The liquid was sweet and cool to Joel's parched throat. "This is great!" he exclaimed.

"Your remedy for weariness?" Mom said with a twinkle.

Joel smiled and ducked his head. "Let's go down to the cave. It's not supper time yet," he said to Elam.

Elam looked questioningly at Mom. "Anything we should be doing in the garden?"

Mom shook her head. "Not now. It really is very warm, and you've worked hard doing the lawn. Here, take some extra cookies with you."

Joel stuck the plastic bag of cookies in his trousers pocket and started out past the barn. To get to what they called "the cave," they had to cross their neighbor John Stanfield's land. An elderly farmer in his sixties, John knew about the cave and didn't mind the boys visiting it.

Soon they came to the creek. After following it a short distance, they came to a place where the creek made a sharp turn. Right at the bend stood a huge old cedar tree. The soil had washed away from its roots. During the summer when the creek was low, there was a lovely open space beneath those gnarled roots, carved out by the swirling, high currents of springtime.

Eagerly, Joel clambered over the roots and dropped down below. "It's completely dry," he called up to Elam. When his brother joined him he added, "Nice and cool, just like I figured. The sun can't reach in here."

They sat back against the earthen walls, munching cookies and listening to the brook babbling just beyond the opening. "I'd almost forgotten how big this cave is," Elam remarked.

"Big enough for ten boys," Joel agreed.

Elam shook his head, considering. "That would be a tight squeeze."

Joel didn't say any more, but he thought, *Maybe someday when we have visitors, I'll bring a bunch of boys down here and show Elam.*

They sat in silence for awhile. Then Elam said, "It worked, didn't it? Mom's remedy for tiredness, I mean."

Joel's thoughts went back over the past few hours. He'd been tired—and unwilling—when they started mowing the lawn. But after Harveys' visit, and that little talk with Mom, he hadn't been tired. He'd been willing! "I guess," he admitted sheepishly.

Thoughtfully, Elam said, "We owe it to Mom to be willing workers."

Joel didn't think he was the only one in need of a little sermon. "And to accept help gratefully," he reminded Elam pointedly.

Now it was Elam's turn to grin sheepishly.

6. A Horse Called Willing

"His name is Will," rumbled Bob Leyland as he climbed from his pickup truck. Bob's deep voice fit his swarthy features and stocky figure exactly.

Joel watched in fascination as Bob went around to the back of his horse trailer and opened the door. "What a name for a horse!" Joel whispered to Elam.

Leyland led the horse outside for everyone to see. Besides the Stutzmans, it seemed the whole Yoder clan had gathered to see the new horse.

Joel drew in his breath sharply. Will was certainly different from Lady. He was bigger for one thing, not taller, but wider. And his hide was such a dark brown it seemed black. Then there was the way he held his head. As a matter of fact, Will didn't seem to hold his head at all. He just let it droop!

Joel glanced at Mom's face. She did not appear too impressed. Harvey, Paul, Joe, Vernon, and Dan were walking around the horse, inspecting him from every angle. Bob Leyland stood with one hand in his pocket and one on Will's halter. "He's quiet," Bob declared. "You couldn't find a quieter horse for a lady to drive."

"Well, that's good," said Harvey, glancing at Mom.

Mom nodded without enthusiasm. Joel smiled. Lady could be quite spirited on the road, and he knew Mom liked it that way.

"I'm willing to let Will board here for several

27

months," Bob went on. Then he smiled broadly. "That reminds me about Will's full name. It's actually . . ." He dug in his pocket and produced a piece of paper. From it he read importantly, "Lansdowne Willing Jaybird the Second!"

The Yoder boys roared with laughter. Elam nudged Joel and hissed, "What a name for a horse, indeed! A horse called Willing!" Joel knew what the nudge was about.

When the laughter died down, Leyland suggested, "Why not take him for a drive?"

With so many helpers, Will was hitched up in a twinkling. First Harvey and the boys piled on the buggy and drove out the lane. When they returned Harvey turned to Mom, "Now you and your boys try him."

Elam and Joel climbed into the buggy with Mom. Joel half-expected one of the men to go along for safety's sake. After all, this was a strange horse. But no one came. Joel could see Elam was pleased.

Mom had the reins. Will was in no hurry at all. Out the lane he walked, plod, plod, plod. Once on the road, Mom urged him to go faster. He jerked up his head. Just lifting his head seemed to take special effort for Will.

"He looks tired," remarked Joel.

Elam disagreed. "He's well-fed and healthy. If you ask me, he's simply unwilling." He chuckled. "Unwilling Will, get up and go!"

Once started, Will trotted quite decently, but only for a short distance. As soon as he dared, he dropped back to a walk.

"We'd have to allow more time to get to places if we kept him," Mom said.

28

"Will we keep him?" asked Elam.

"I don't know. It may well be the best we can expect for a loaner. Leyland wouldn't want to loan us his best horses, anyway."

Elam nodded. He could see that Mom was right. "Maybe Joel could teach Will to be more willing too," he suggested, with a sly glance at his brother.

Joel gave him a playful shove. "Now, boys," Mom said. She turned Will around and headed back to the waiting group of men.

"What do you think?" Harvey asked as Mom climbed from the buggy.

"He seems to be very quiet," Mom replied.

"He is," Leyland assured her. "Will has no surprises for you. Board him, and he's yours to use, free of charge, for a couple of months."

"That's very reasonable," said Harvey.

Mom nodded. "We'll take him, and thank you very much."

The Yoder boys unhitched Will and led him to the barn. Joel trailed after them. He wanted to see what Lady thought of the new horse.

Lady was lying down in her stall but scrambled to her feet when Paul led Will into the stall next to hers. She put her nose across the partition and gave a questioning little whinny. Will whinnied back in a friendly way.

"They'll get along," Joe said reassuringly. Then he smiled, "With a name like his, your new horse should be a willing worker when it comes to cultivating the garden."

"I wonder," said Elam. "He certainly didn't seem very willing on the road."

"When do you expect to be cultivating again?" Joe

wanted to know.

Elam thought for a moment. "Tomorrow, I think."

"Well, I could come over and help you get started," Joe offered, "just in case Will makes any trouble. He may never have pulled a cultivator before."

"Oh, I think . . ." Elam paused. Then he said, "All right. Thanks."

"Starting in the morning? See you then." Joe left the barn and headed for home, following his brothers across the field.

"I really don't think he needs to come," Elam said to Joel.

Joel said nothing, but he was glad Joe was coming. With a new horse, there was no knowing what might happen in the garden.

But the next morning Will was quite docile as Joe helped Elam hitch him to the cultivator. With Joe leading him, Will plodded up and down several rows. Joel compared the lazy way Will lifted his feet to Lady's eager steps. Either Will was tired, Joel thought . . . or he was unwilling!

Then suddenly, Will stopped. One moment he was moving; the next he wasn't! There he stood, halfway down a row, head down, feet rooted to the ground. He did not seem to hear Elam calling, "Giddap!" He did not seem to feel Joe tugging at his bridle. He had simply stopped.

Elam took out a handkerchief and wiped the sweat from his face. "You need some of Mom's remedy for tiredness, I think," he said to Will.

Joel felt his face grow hot. Somehow it embarrassed him to see this horse acting so unwillingly. Was that the way he looked when he was tired of working?

30

"We'll beat him at his own game," said Joe. He sat down on the ground near Will. Elam did the same. Will turned his head and looked at them.

After awhile, Joe said, "He'll get tired of standing there. Pretty soon he'll start off, then we must be ready to go too!"

But Joe was wrong. Will did not start off. It was the boys who got tired of waiting. Soon Elam was back at the handles of the cultivator, and Joe had hold of Will's bridle. "Okay," Joe said loudly in his most grown-up voice, "Lansdowne Willing Jaybird the Second—GET OUT OF HERE!"

But Will did not move.

Joe was becoming irritated. "Bring me a stick, Joel," he commanded.

Joel's heart lurched. He knew how Mom felt about beating a horse. She would never even touch Lady with a stick. What would Mom do with unwilling Will?

"Can you find a stick?" Joe repeated impatiently.

Joel looked around halfheartedly. Then he spied Mom coming down the row toward them. Had she heard Joe?

If she had, she gave no sign. All she said was, "Here, try this." And she held a carrot just out of reach of Will's nose.

Will's drooping eyes opened wide. He stretched out his nose. Mom kept the carrot out of reach. Will took a step forward, then another, and another. "You take the carrot," Mom said to Joe.

Joe smiled sheepishly and took the carrot. "Well, well," he said as Will continued plodding obediently down the row. "So it takes a carrot to make you live up to your name!"

7. Visitors

One warm day followed another. Mom kept saying the weather was unusually warm for June. But every now and then a little shower kept the soil in the garden from drying up.

The warm weather was just right for Pat the pig. He didn't need to spend his nights in the kitchen any more. Elam and Joel built a little pen for him in the woodshed. They had considered returning him to the barn, but he still needed to be fed so often that it was more convenient to have him nearby.

"I'm glad we don't have to bottle-feed him anymore," Joel said one morning as Elam and he stood watching the pig slurp milk from his trough.

"Why? I thought you said it was fun."

Joel shrugged. "It was fun, maybe. But I got tired of it."

"You're always getting tired of things," Elam accused.

"Not any more than you!" Joel answered hotly.

A bright little-girl voice chirped behind them, "Hi there!"

Joel whirled. There stood the four youngest Yoders, except for the baby. Dorcas and Ruth each held onto a little brother's hand. Amos was five and Adam was three.

Joel couldn't think of anything to say. His face burned. The newcomers had probably heard him and Elam quarreling.

Dorcas held out a folded piece of paper. "We brought a note for your mom. Lizzie couldn't come. She's busy helping Mom get ready for company."

"Company?" asked Joel curiously. "On a Saturday?"

"Out-of-state visitors. From Ohio!" Dorcas announced importantly. "They're coming for dinner today. And you're invited too!"

"We? Why?" asked Elam in surprise.

"Yes. That's what this letter is about. Where's your mom?" questioned Dorcas.

"Inside. Come on." Joel led the way to the kitchen. Mom smiled as she greeted their little visitors. Then she opened the letter, and everybody was quiet as she read it.

Soon Mom looked up at the boys. "Ready to go away for dinner? To Harveys?"

"Why are we invited?" Elam wondered. "Is the company somebody we know?"

"Yes. Well, no, most of the folks are strangers— except for the one woman, Wilma Detweiler. I went to school with her." She smiled at Dorcas and Ruth, "I guess your mom knew that."

"The Detweilers are Mom's cousins," Dorcas explained.

Mom nodded. "There will be three Detweiler families in the van, I understand."

Dorcas nodded back. She obviously felt quite grown-up having this discussion with Joel's mom. "Three brothers. All my mom's cousins." She paused. "Can you come for dinner, then?"

"Yes. Thank you for inviting us."

"Then we must hurry home. Come, Adam. Amos,

where are you?"

"The boys and Joel went out to the pig again," Elam mumbled. He watched through the open doorway as Dorcas gathered up the younger children and herded them out the lane. "She's like a mother hen with chicks," he remarked to Mom.

"Who is?" Mom asked absently.

"Dorcas," Elam replied. "See, there she goes with her brood."

"Oh, I see," Mom said. Her mind seemed somewhere else. Then her voice grew businesslike. "Where's Joel? You boys should get washed up and put on clean clothes."

"Do we have to go?" Elam wanted to know.

Mom looked at him in surprise.

"I mean," he said hastily, "it's just a bunch of strange grown-ups. . . ."

"Not just grown-ups," Mom interrupted. "There are at least two boys along, and some girls. You could all play a game together after dinner."

"Boys my age?" Elam asked, his voice brightening.

"I think so. Now please find Joel and go wash up."

The hot sun was almost directly overhead as the three Stutzmans walked over to Harveys. Sweat formed under Joel's hatband and ran down his face. "Must be ninety degrees," he remarked.

Elam didn't hear him. He was staring in fascination at all the strangers on the Yoders' porch and front lawn. Men, women, boys, and girls seemed to be everywhere.

But Elsie Yoder managed to squeeze everybody around her long kitchen table for the meal. Joel found himself tucked between two strange boys.

Every now and then he stole a glance at them as he ate. The color of their hair fascinated him. He had never seen reddish-brown hair like that.

"Oops," he said as his right elbow bumped the one boy's arm.

"Sorry," the boy mumbled back, his mouth full of potatoes and roast beef. "It's because I'm left-handed. Doesn't work out too well when the table's full like this."

"Never mind," Joel said. He kept his elbow tucked in after that. He wondered what the boy's name was.

After dinner the schoolboys went outdoors. They sat on the grass in the shade of the maple tree and looked shyly at one another. Besides the red-haired boys, there was one other, a thin, pale boy who wore glasses.

It was the pale boy who spoke first. "I'm Lester Detweiler. What are your names?" his eyes were on Elam and Joel.

Joel looked at Elam, waiting for him to say something. "I'm Elam Stutzman," said Elam.

Joel had hoped he'd say, "And this is my brother Joel." But he didn't, so Joel said in a small voice, "I'm Joel."

"Joel who?" demanded the smaller of the red-haired boys.

Joel jerked his thumb towards Elam. "I'm his brother."

The red-haired boy nodded. "I'm Allan Detweiler. This is my brother, Aaron." He nudged the bigger red-haired boy, who smiled amiably. Joel wondered why the younger boy had spoken first.

"We're first cousins, Aaron and Allan and I,"

Lester explained.

"Where do you live?" asked Allan loudly.

"Right over there in that house," Elam said, pointing across the field.

Lester had a bright idea. "Maybe we could go and see your place while the grown-ups sit and visit?"

"If you like," Elam said politely.

"Aw, it's too warm to walk around much," Allan protested.

Suddenly Joel remembered the cave. It would be cool there. He also remembered that he wanted to see how many boys could get into it. Forgetting his shyness, he said eagerly, "We could go to our cave! It's nice and cool in there."

Allan looked at him with new interest. "Your cave? Where is it?"

Lester was already unfolding his long legs to get up. "I'll go in and ask my mom or dad whether we can go."

Within minutes he was back wearing a smile. "They said to be back in an hour."

Joel and the others scrambled to their feet as well, and ignoring the hot sun, they trotted across the field.

8. Sold for Pet Food

"Let's go to the house first," Elam suggested, leading the way.

"Do you want to see our pet pig?" Joel asked.

"A pet pig?" exclaimed Allan. "Whoever heard of keeping a pig for a pet!"

Joel wished he had not mentioned Pat, but there was no turning back now. Sheepishly he opened the woodshed door. "There she is."

"A pet pig? In the house?" Allan said in disbelief.

But his older brother was very interested. Aaron lingered near the pig's pen and spoke to Pat in a friendly voice. Joel decided then and there he liked Aaron better than Allan.

Soon Allan called, "Come on, Aaron. We're going to the cave now."

Joel was puzzled as he tramped down to the creek with the others. Wasn't Aaron the older of the two red-haired boys? He certainly was taller. But he didn't act older. In fact, he didn't seem to mind being bossed around by his younger brother. Joel was sure Elam would mind!

"Here we are," Elam said, climbing down the creek bank.

"Where's the cave? I don't see any cave." The demanding note was back in Allan's voice.

"Come on down here," Lester told him.

One by one they scrambled down and entered the

cool hollow between the roots of the cedar. Allan took a look around and declared, "This isn't a very big cave."

The words hurt Joel almost as though Allan had hit him. His hands balled up into tight fists. But after a moment he unclenched them again. It would never do to hit a visitor.

"It's nice and cool," Lester said pleasantly. Aaron only smiled.

Everyone sat down on the hard-packed earth except Allan. He remained standing, hunching his shoulders beneath the low ceiling. "My good pants would get dirty," he said.

Joel was not surprised when Allan demanded, "How long are we going to stay here?"

"We can leave now if you like," Elam replied evenly. Joel was quite irritated, but he admired Elam for keeping his voice calm.

"Could we see your barn yet?" Lester asked as they emerged into the bright sunlight again.

Joel wanted to say, "Let's not bother." He could imagine Allan making fun of Lady and Will and Porker. He wasn't sure he could bear it.

But Elam said, "Sure," and they all trooped up to the barn. Soon they stood in front of the horses' stalls.

"What are their names?" demanded Allan.

I won't tell him, Joel thought. But Elam answered politely, "This one is Lady. She's lame, so we borrowed that one for a while. He's called Will."

Aaron had been staring at the dark horse. Now he exclaimed, "Will?" His voice was high, almost squeaky.

Aaron stepped closer to the stall. Eagerly he

reached out and touched the horse's nose. "Will? Do you mean Lansdowne Willing Jaybird the Second?" Joel was dumbfounded. "How did you know?"

"We had him! We had him for six years!" Aaron was so excited his voice squeaked even more. "He was Mom's horse. She drove him a lot. She liked him." Aaron paused, his voice strangely sad. "I liked him too."

"I didn't!" Allan hooted. "Will was as slow as molasses in January. I thought he went for pet food when we sent him away."

Aaron shook his head happily as he patted Will's nose again and again. "But he didn't. He didn't go for pet food. He came here!" His voice was full of wonder.

Elam was amazed. "Isn't that a coincidence! You boys came here almost by accident, and here is your old horse!"

Allan seemed embarrassed by the fuss his brother was making over Will. He turned and looked at the empty stalls near Lady. "Where are your work horses? Out in the pasture?"

Joel squirmed. Why did Allan have to ask that? Now he would find out—oh, he would find out many things Joel felt Allan Detweiler need not know.

Elam was still polite. "We haven't any work horses. Harvey Yoders farm our place."

Allan's eyebrows shot up. "Why?"

"Oh," said Elam quietly. "Maybe you haven't heard. Our father died when we were little."

Joel didn't see how Elam could say it so quietly and matter-of-factly.

For once, Allan didn't know what to say. He just stood there, looking first at Elam and then at Joel.

39

His face had turned white.

It was Aaron who stammered, "You—you don't have a father? And we—we don't have a mother. She died two years ago."

If Elam's words had been like a bombshell dropped in their midst, Aaron's were even more so. Joel could feel his anger toward Allan draining away. In its place came a feeling of sympathy. No mother! He couldn't imagine how that would be. Somehow, it hadn't occurred to him that a mother could die too. Mothers were . . . well, mothers were just always there. At least, his mother was.

The silence in the barn had grown strained. Nobody knew what to say.

Then Will gave a short whinny, and Aaron turned to pet him again. Joel watched him and thought, *No wonder he liked that horse. It was the horse his mother drove.* He cleared his throat. "You were sorry to see Will go?"

"Yes," said Aaron. "Yes." There was a catch in his voice.

"Will wasn't any good," Allan spat out. He turned on his heel. "I guess it's time we get back to the Yoders. We're leaving to visit some other places before supper time."

The others had to hurry to catch up with him. Joel fell into step beside Aaron. "Who—who does the housekeeping for you?" he asked hesitantly.

"Aunt Lena. And we have two big sisters," Aaron replied sadly. Joel wondered whether he was thinking of his dead mother, or because he was sorry to leave Will.

"We won't need Will much longer, because Lady will be well soon. Then you could have Will back if you like," Joel said generously.

Aaron shook his head sadly. "Dad wouldn't want him. Will was too slow. That's why he sold him for pet food."

"I can't understand how Bob Leyland got hold of Will," Joel puzzled.

"Neither can I," a slow smile spread across Aaron's face. "But I'm glad he did. I'm glad Will wasn't turned into pet food."

9. The Detweiler Boys Again

There were so many things to talk about at the supper table that the boys almost forgot to eat. "Mom, did you know that Aaron and Allan don't have any mother?" asked Joel.

"Yes, I knew."

"Why didn't you tell us?"

"I don't know. I guess I forgot," Mom replied.

"And Will was their horse once! Would you believe that?" Elam exclaimed.

Mom looked up from her plate. "That's interesting. Did they like him?"

"Aaron did. And his mother did too. But Allan and his dad didn't. So they sold Will for pet food."

"H-m-m," said Mom thoughtfully. "For pet food? It makes me wonder what kind of a horse dealer Leyland is."

"Maybe not too trustworthy," Elam remarked.

"Trustworthy or not, he provided us with a horse," Mom pointed out. "And tomorrow we use the horse to go to church for the first time."

Elam gave a little groan. "And church is way over at Chris Leimbachs. That's more than four miles. With a horse like Will, we'll have to start off half an hour earlier than usual to get there on time!"

"So we shall!" Mom said briskly. "It's still better than walking."

"I'm not so sure," Elam said darkly. After cultivating

the garden with an unwilling horse several times, he could understand why the Detweilers had gotten rid of Will.

Mom ignored his grumbling and looked at the clock. "We'd better get started with our Saturday evening chores," she exclaimed. "Early to bed and early to rise . . . and early to church!"

"Early to start off, late to get there," Elam corrected.

Mom smiled. "Be that as it may, we shall do our best."

As it turned out, they were ready to start off next morning a full three-quarters of an hour earlier than they ordinarily would have left for Leimbachs. Surprisingly enough, Will trotted along briskly.

"What's gotten into him? He's actually holding up his head," Elam remarked.

"Maybe he's still happy because he saw Aaron yesterday," suggested Joel. "They seemed to be good friends."

"Huh," said Elam.

"Why not?" Joel said defensively, "We're good friends with Lady."

"This horse is different," Elam persisted.

"So is Aaron," Joel pointed out. He turned to Mom. "Did you notice Aaron? He seems sort of quiet."

Mom nodded. "I talked with his Aunt Lena about Aaron. He . . . well, he's thirteen, isn't he?"

"I think so," replied Elam.

"His Aunt Lena says he has the mind of a seven- or eight-year-old. He hasn't gotten much further than third grade at school."

"Oh," said Joel in surprise. "So it's like he's actually younger than I am?"

"In some ways. In other ways people like Aaron can be quite wise. For instance, Aaron is very good with animals. He seems to have a special way with them," Mom explained.

Their conversation was interrupted when they came to the busy county road. Mom brought Will to a full stop and looked both ways to check the traffic. Then she slapped the reins on Will's back. "Giddap!"

Joel gripped the armrest of the buggy. A car was coming over the hill. Couldn't Will move a little faster as they crossed the road? Then they were across, and Joel relaxed again. His thoughts turned back to Aaron. Learning about his handicap hadn't made Joel like him any less. *I still like Aaron better than Allan. At least Aaron doesn't make fun of things,* Joel thought.

With Will more lively, the Stutzmans reached Chris Leimbachs before anyone else! Joel went with Elam as he unhitched Will and tied him in the barn. Then they wandered over to the big shed where the church benches were set up. "Lots of room today," Joel remarked.

"It's a good thing with those visitors from Ohio here too." Elam pointed. The big van that had brought the Detweilers to Harveys yesterday was driving in the lane.

"So they're here too!" Joel said in surprise.

"Of course," Elam said. "Why would they come all the way from Ohio and not stay over Sunday?"

Joel nodded. It had not occurred to him that he would ever again see Aaron and Allan. Yet there they were, red hair and all, climbing out of the van.

44

Joel hung back. He really didn't want to meet Allan.

But the Detweiler boys, along with Lester, made a beeline for Elam and Joel. Lester's eyes were friendly behind his glasses. "Good to see you again. I liked your cave. It was nice and cool."

Allan said nothing, but Joel thought he heard him sniff.

"Did you come with Will?" Aaron asked, that slow grin spreading across his face again.

"Yes, and he hurried this morning," Joel said enthusiastically.

"He could when he wanted to," Aaron said.

Elam chuckled, "When he was willing, you mean?"

Aaron nodded. "That's right. When he was willing. Can we go say 'Hi' to Will before church starts?"

"Sure. Come on," Joel said. He and Aaron moved away from the other three. Soon the thirteen-year-old was talking to Will and stroking his nose. The look in Will's eyes was unmistakably happy! And when it was time for the boys to go into the shed, Will gave a low, sorrowful nicker.

Soon the shed was echoing to the slow strains of the *Loblied,* as the congregation sang, "Oh, God Father, we praise Thee . . ." Joel sang too. He didn't know all the church tunes, but the *Loblied* he knew because it was the second song they sang at every service.

He tried to pay careful attention to the minister. Mom would ask them tonight what Scriptures had been read. Some Sundays he simply didn't catch on, but today he did. It was Matthew, Chapter 5. Joel tried not to fidget. Sitting for hours on a backless bench was hard.

By the time church was over, Joel was very hungry! Eagerly he went with the other boys to the house where lunch was laid out on long tables. He spread thick slices of homemade bread lavishly with butter and jam. Crunchy pickles and carrot sticks went well with the sandwiches. For dessert there were several kinds of sweet, spicy cookies. Church lunches were never fancy meals, but to Joel they were always the best food in the world!

After lunch the schoolboys drifted together in a little group on the lawn. Usually everybody was talkative because they knew each other well. Today they were quieter, and Joel knew it was because of the Detweiler boys.

But Edwin Miller, who was in Elam's grade at school, could never be quiet for long. He started talking about horses. Most of the boys joined in, telling about their work horses and their driving horses.

"Have you heard what the Stutzmans' new horse is called?" Allan Detweiler spoke up. "His name is Willing, but he's the most unwilling horse you ever saw. I know, because we had him for awhile too."

Anger boiled up inside Joel. It wasn't that Allan's words weren't true, but his voice was so scornful, like yesterday.

Afterwards, Joel couldn't understand why he did it. He didn't think about it at all—it just happened. He stepped toward Allan and swung his fist, thumping him on the arm. "Don't talk about our horse that way!" he said heatedly.

Allan jerked around in surprise. "Why did you do that? I was just telling the truth."

46

Before Joel could say anything more, Elam piped up, "Never mind my little brother. He can get real heated up about nothing at all."

Joel glared at Elam. Then he walked away from the group of boys, his hands stuffed into his pockets and tears running down his face. He felt awful.

Someone followed him. It was Aaron, his face full of concern. "Shall we go talk to Will?" he asked.

Joel shrugged. "I don't care." He trailed after Aaron to where Will was tied up. In a minute or two, a smile crept to Joel's lips. Who could help smiling, the way that boy and that horse talked to each other?

10. The Heavenly Father

Just as Joel expected, Elam lost no time telling Mom about the incident at church. After they were in the buggy heading for home, he announced, "Joel punched Allan Detweiler today!"

"You hit a visitor?" Mom was shocked.

Joel's face burned. "Allan kept making fun of our horse."

"He wasn't really making fun of Will. Just stating facts," objected Elam.

"I see," said Mom quietly.

"Allan made fun of our things yesterday too! I just don't like him. He . . . he's so proud," Joel said hotly.

"Oh," said Mom. "But Aaron isn't?"

"No. I like him. He's nice." Joel waited for Mom to scold him.

But Mother didn't scold. Instead, she was very quiet all the way home. It made Joel uncomfortable. He preferred a scolding to not knowing what Mom was thinking.

That evening during devotions Mom said, "I'll read the last part of the chapter we had today." And she began, "'Ye have heard that it hath been said, Thou shalt love thy neighbour, and hate thine enemy. But I say unto you, Love your enemies, bless them that curse you, do good to them that hate you, and pray for them which despitefully use you, and persecute you; That ye may be the children of your

Father which is in heaven. . . .'"

When Mom looked up, she repeated softly, "'Love your enemies, bless them that curse you, do good to them that hate you.'"

Joel squirmed.

"Joel," Mom said pointedly, "Allan may not have been very nice. But does that excuse you for being mean to him?"

"No," mumbled Joel.

Mom looked at the Bible again. "I like this line: 'That ye may be children of your Father which is in heaven.' God really is our Father, you know. And—have you thought about it? Children are like their fathers and mothers. They look like them. They act like them. If we are children of our heavenly Father, we do as He does. We love our enemies and do good to them that hate us."

Joel and Elam both nodded. For a few moments the only sound in the kitchen was the clock ticking. Then Mom said, "Joel, not having an earthly father can make us feel we're . . . that we're different from others. It can cause us to get offended too easily. We're too quick to think people are making fun of us, simply because we feel so different."

Joel shrugged. He had never thought about it that way, but Mom was probably right. He knew he often wished he had a daddy like other boys.

"It might help you to remember," Mom went on, "that we do, indeed, have a Father in heaven. And He is everybody's Father. Yours. Aaron's. Allan's. He loves us all, and He wants us all to love each other."

Mom waited. Joel knew she expected him to say something, so he said, "Yes, Mom." He was still wondering whether he was going to get punished for

49

punching Allan when Mom abruptly changed the subject. "Did Aaron want to see Will again today?"

"Oh, yes!" exclaimed Joel. "I think he would have spent all afternoon with Will. He loves that horse."

"I talked with Aaron's Aunt Lena again after church," Mom said. "She had hoped they would keep Will for Aaron's sake, but Aaron's dad saw no reason to keep a horse that wasn't much use."

"Too bad Aaron had to lose his mother and his horse," Joel said sympathetically.

"I know," Mom agreed. "I think maybe Aaron's dad just didn't realize how it was for Aaron." She turned and looked at the clock. "Past bedtime, boys."

Joel got to his feet reluctantly. Tired though he was, he never liked going to bed!

"Joel," said Mom.

"Yes?"

"In a week or two, I want you and Elam to write the Detweiler boys. You can write friendly letters, with a bit of news and a thank-you for their visit. And, Joel, I want you to apologize for hitting Allan."

Joel's heart plummeted to his shoes. He turned and walked slowly to the stairs. He did not want to write to Allan Detweiler!

"Joel?" Mom's voice followed him, demanding an answer.

"Yes, Mom."

Strawberry-picking was in full swing now. Joel and Elam were kept very busy helping Mom with their eight long rows of berries. About half the berries went to customers who came right to the Stutzman farm. The rest were picked up by the wholesale truck that went through the area each morning on its way to the fruit and vegetable market in the big city. Elam and Joel had to get up at the crack of dawn in order to have dozens of quarts of berries ready for the truck.

"I like early-morning picking the best," Elam remarked to Joel one forenoon after the wholesale truck had gone, and they were back in the patch picking for other customers.

"Why?" asked Joel.

"Because it's nice and cool then. By this time of day the sun gets warm."

"Not just warm—hot!" grumbled Joel. "I feel half-baked. And my back hurts. And we still have three rows for today!"

Elam threw him an irritating grin. "Maybe it's time you had a chat with Lansdowne Willing Jaybird the S—"

"Oh, stop that!" snapped Joel. "I'm tired of hearing about being willing."

"You're tired? But I thought Mom said willingness is a rem—"

"I said, 'Stop it'!" Joel shouted. He covered his ears with his hands.

Mom's voice floated to them from two rows over. "Quiet, boys. Somebody's here, a customer, probably."

Elam squinted at the red vehicle coming in the lane. "No, I think that's Mr. Duval's jeep. Remember? He promised to come and check on Lady after a few weeks."

Joel was on his feet in an instant. "We'd better go to the barn to find out what he has to say."

Mom smiled. "It will give us all a break from

51

berry-picking."

Mr. Duval was already in Lady's stall by the time they reached the barn. Carefully the vet removed the splint and ran his hand up and down the injured leg. Lady turned her head and watched him warily.

Mr. Duval straightened up to find the three Stutzmans watching him. "Hi," he said briefly. "The leg is doing well, so she can do without the splint. And she can go to pasture now, but not before you have filled in any groundhog burrows!"

"All right," Elam promised gravely.

"Good," said Mr. Duval. "I'll be back to check her before you take her on the road." With that, he left the barn and hurried to his jeep.

"Mom, shall we start right away?" Joel asked eagerly.

"Start what?"

"Filling in the groundhog holes!" Joel replied impatiently.

Elam hooted, "Listen to the boy who was so tired a few minutes ago! Now he wants to start lugging around a ton or two of gravel!"

"Elam. Don't tease," Mom warned. Turning to Joel she added, "I'm afraid we'll have to keep at those berries today."

"But Lady wants to go out to the pasture," protested Joel.

Mom smiled. "She's quite contented here. I doubt she understood Mr. Duval when he said she may go out. Do you think so?"

Grudgingly, Joel shook his head. He could hardly wait to race down the pasture with Jim and Lady once more. Will had been in the field a few times, but he didn't like running there any better than on the road. He just stood around eating grass. Joel was sure Lady longed to be outdoors too!

But the berries came first. Feet dragging, Joel followed the others to the garden.

11. Letters to the Detweilers

There had been no rain for a week. Because they didn't have full-scale irrigation equipment, Mom and the boys watered the berry patch to keep it from drying up. Soon the berries grew smaller. The wholesale truck stopped coming because only large berries were wanted at the city market.

"That means we get to can a lot of little berries ourselves this year," Mom said cheerfully.

Joel groaned, though not too loudly. He really did want to be a willing worker. But he knew that now they would have to hull the berries as well as pick them. "When will we ever have time to get the pasture ready for Lady?" he complained. "It's just berries, berries, berries all the time. Watering them. Picking them. And now, hulling and canning them!"

"The berry season will soon be past," Mom assured him.

Joel was not so sure. Still, he began to work with a will. Maybe if they picked and hulled very fast, there would be time tonight to haul some gravel. As he moved up the berry row, he said to himself, "One good thing about being so busy—Mom hasn't said anything more about writing to the Detweilers. Maybe she'll forget all about it."

There was no time for anything but berries that day. But the next day, they were through by mid-afternoon because a lady bought all the little berries for making jam. They wouldn't have to hull those!

Mom smiled at Joel. "I don't have to ask what you plan to do!"

Joel smiled back. "I know a place where there's some gravel on the creek bank. Shall we use the wagon or wheelbarrow to haul some to that groundhog burrow?"

"The play wagon would be easier," Elam said as he headed for the woodshed where the wagon was kept.

Joel glanced briefly into Pat's pen. It was empty now. Pat had been moved out to the barn. The once-runty pig was now just as round and healthy as the other weaned pigs.

"There's another job we're supposed to do," Elam remarked. "Mom said we ought to tear out that pig-pen again."

"Lady comes first!" cried Joel, grabbing the wagon and trotting over the lawn.

Hauling loads of gravel uphill was backbreaking work. "This groundhog burrow must be really deep," Joel said after they had shoveled the third load into the hole.

Elam grinned. "Maybe it's a bottomless pit. Maybe the hole goes right through the middle of the earth. Maybe this gravel we're shoveling is coming out on the other side of the world, in China or somewhere!"

"Oh, you," Joel shot back. He took the wagon and headed for the creek. He was tired, but he wasn't going to admit it!

Both boys were bent down, shoveling, when they heard someone calling, "What are you fellows doing?"

55

Edwin Miller was standing on the opposite bank of the creek with a fishing rod balanced on his shoulder. The Millers were not close neighbors to the Stutzmans, but this same creek ran through their farm. Edwin had followed the creek all the way from his home. "Need any help?" he called.

"Sure do!" Elam called back.

Edwin rolled up his pants' legs and splashed across the creek. "Hauling gravel for your driveway or something?"

"No," chuckled Elam. He grabbed the wagon handle and strained to pull it up the hill. Edwin dropped his fishing pole and pushed from behind. Elam puffed, "We're filling in a groundhog burrow, so Lady doesn't hurt herself again."

"I see," said Edwin, puffing too. This load was also quickly swallowed up by the hole. Edwin looked around. "We could use stones too, couldn't we, from that pile over by the fence?"

Joel agreed enthusiastically, "That's a good idea. Stones would fill it up faster. And they would be harder for the groundhog to move, if he ever got it into his head to open the burrow again."

They headed over to the fence with the wagon and were soon back with a load of stones. After several such loads, Elam said finally, "Now let's go and get Lady!"

Edwin looked at his watch. "I think I have time to stay till you've brought her out. I would like to see her too. She will be glad to stretch her legs, I'd guess."

Jim had been frolicking around the boys as they worked. Now he pricked up his ears and barked.

Joel laughed. "You heard us talking about Lady,

didn't you? Would you like to race with her again? Maybe you can win a race with her now. She won't be running very fast today."

"She'd better take it easy at first," Elam agreed as they all hurried to the barn. Lady nickered happily as Elam untied her and led her outdoors. Her nostrils flared as she took in the fresh air. Once in the pasture, she reared up her head and began to run. It was not a full gallop. It wasn't even a fast trot. But Lady was running, and she was glad. So was Jim! So were Elam, Joel, and Edwin! Laughing and shouting, they ran after the horse and the dog, right down to the creek. The muscles that ached from hauling stones were quite forgotten.

"I better go," Edwin said, rolling up his trousers' legs again. He picked up his fishing pole and stepped into the water.

"Good-bye, and thanks for your help!" called Elam.

"Good thing he came along when he did, or we'd still be hauling gravel," Joel remarked as they trudged uphill together.

Supper was ready when they got to the house. After they started eating, Joel asked, "Mom, does Will go back to Bob Leyland as soon as we can use Lady again?"

Mom hesitated. "I . . . I don't know. I keep remembering how much Aaron Detweiler liked Will. And I can't bear to think of Will going for pet food."

"What will you do? Wrap Will up in shiny paper, tie him with a fancy ribbon, and send him back to the Detweilers as a gift?" Elam teased.

Mom answered, "Of course we couldn't do that. But we . . . well, I need time to think it over. And besides, we still need Will. Mr. Duval hasn't pronounced Lady roadworthy yet." Mom paused, then went on briskly, "Speaking of the Detweilers . . . that reminds me, Joel. There is a letter you need to write. Tonight."

Joel groaned inwardly. *I should never have mentioned Will*, he thought. *Now I'll have to write that dreadful letter.*

There was no way around it. After chores Mom brought out paper and pens. Elam started writing with a flourish. Joel watched him enviously for a moment. Elam had it easy. He didn't need to write an apology.

"Write about other things first," Mom prompted Joel gently. "Remember to thank them for the visit. At the end, say you're sorry."

Joel nodded. He nibbled the end of his pencil. He wrote:

> Dear Aaron and Allan,
> Greetings across the miles. We have been busy picking berries. Are you making hay on your farm? Today we filled in the . . .

He stopped. No, he wasn't going to write to Allan about horses. Not a word. He erased that sentence again, and wrote some more about berry-picking.

Then he started a new paragraph.

> Thank you for visiting us. I am sorry I hit you at church that day.

Joel looked up and asked, "How shall I end my letter?"

"The usual way. You learned about letter-writing at school, didn't you? "Sincerely" or "yours truly" should be fine," Mom replied.

Joel thought it over. "Yours truly" did not sound right. He did not feel "yours truly" towards Allan Detweiler. "Sincerely" would be okay. He wrote:

> Sincerely,
> Joel Stutzman

Joel looked across at Elam. He had finished too. "May I read your letter?" Joel asked.

"Sure. If I may read yours."

Joel shoved his across the table and took Elam's. He frowned as he read it. Elam, of course, had written all about Lady getting better and about filling up the groundhog hole. About Will, Elam had written:

> Mom hasn't decided whether we will keep him or not. He's not much of a horse, and yet we have gotten sort of fond of him. He would be gentle enough for Joel to learn to drive.

Joel scowled at his brother. "You didn't need to write all that."

"Why not?" Elam asked innocently. "I had to write something. Aaron will be happy to read about Will."

"That's right," Joel agreed. He hadn't been thinking about Aaron as he wrote, only about Allan. "Mom? Are you going to proofread them too?"

Mom read them and smiled at Joel. "I hope this helps you do as the Scriptures say. You know . . . Love your enemy."

Joel said nothing. He wasn't sure he was any closer to loving Allan Detweiler.

12. A Heavy Load

The late-season strawberries were not finished bearing when the peas started. At first, Joel thought picking peas was fun. It was fun to rustle through the dewy vines hunting for the fattest pods. It was fun to see how fast you could fill up a six-quart or bushel basket.

But after a few days the fun wore off. Soon it was easier to complain than to pick peas. "It's so hard to find them," Joel grumbled to Elam one morning. "Everything's green—the vines, the leaves, the pods. With strawberries, at least the ripe ones are a different color."

"Uh-oh! Getting tired already?" Elam asked. "We still have five rows to go."

Joel groaned, "Five whole rows? Why, we'll never get done!"

"What's the rush? What is it you'd rather be doing?" Elam asked in his irritating way.

"Helping make hay," Joel answered promptly. He sat back on his heels and stared longingly at the field beside the garden. Two mowers were clickety-clacking through the sweet-smelling clover, laying it flat in straight swaths. Joe and Vernon Yoder were the privileged fellows driving the teams. "I wish I could do that," Joel said wistfully.

"Even if we were farming, you wouldn't be old enough to drive a team and mower," Elam pointed out quickly.

"Okay, but I could drive a team with a hay wagon," Joel shot back.

The boys had been speaking so loudly that Mom heard them where she was picking late-bearing strawberries. "Maybe you will get a chance to drive a team this summer," she reminded Joel. "Remember we told Harvey he may ask for help if he needs it."

"Not much chance that he'll need help, with four boys of his own," Joel mumbled.

Suddenly Elam jumped up. "There goes the mailman! My turn to get the mail!" He dashed across the garden, taking great leaps across the rows of vegetables.

Joel wailed after him, "No, it's my turn! You fetched the mail two days in a row. Come back, Elam!"

Elam appeared not to hear him and kept right on going.

Joel was almost in tears. "Mom, it really is my turn. Elam got the mail on Monday and Tuesday—remember? Yesterday and today are my days."

Mom's eyes followed Elam, who by this time was halfway out the lane. "I guess you're right, but Elam didn't seem to remember that. Well, Joel, I'll tell Elam that it will be your turn tomorrow and Monday."

"Okay," said Joel grumpily. He found himself wanting to shout angrily at Elam when he came back with the mail.

Mom guessed his feelings. "Joel, you must not be angry at Elam. I will remind him, and you stay quiet."

"Okay," said Joel again. He contented himself with glowering at Elam while Mom rebuked him.

Elam ducked his head. "I forgot that you get two days."

"Apologize," came Mom's firm reminder.

"I'm sorry," said Elam, none too willingly.

Mom was still looking at him. "Remember, an apology isn't real unless we mean it."

"Yes, Mom," Elam muttered. Then he held up an envelope. "See? There's a letter for me and Joel from the Detweiler boys."

Joel jumped up excitedly. "There is? Let me see it."

Elam held the letter out of his reach. "I didn't think you would want to see it. You sure weren't very enthusiastic about writing to Allan."

"Getting a letter is more fun than writing one. Let me see it!" Joel insisted.

"Open the envelope," said Mom sternly. "Perhaps there are two letters, one from Aaron and one from Allan."

Elam slit the envelope and peered inside. "Yep, there are two sheets. This one must be from Aaron." He held up a paper covered with a large, childish scrawl.

"Let me have one!" demanded Joel.

There was an edge to their mother's voice. "Joel! Remember to say please. And Elam, don't tease."

Joel looked at her and began to laugh. "You made a poem, Mom."

Mom smiled slightly. "So I did. Just don't forget what I'm saying."

Elam handed Aaron's letter to Joel, and Joel began to read:

Dear Joel and Elam,

Thank you for your letters. We are all OK. How is Will? Do you cultivate the gardon with him? I wod like to see Will again. Dad dosent let me drive our horses on the road, but if I had Will, I think I coud drive him. Say hi to Will for me.

From your friend Aaron Detweiler

"His letter is all full of Will," chuckled Joel. "He just can't forget that horse. Too bad his dad won't buy him, because we won't need Will much longer anymore."

Mom looked at him. "Oh, but maybe we do need him. Will would be just the horse for a young boy like you to learn to drive on the road. Here, do you want to read Allan's letter yet too?"

Joel took the letter. Allan's handwriting was neat—much neater than Joel's.

Dear Joel and Elam,
How are you? I am fine. Thanks for your letters. We had an interesting trip that time but I was glad to come home again. We are busy with the hay. My sisters help too, so we have enough help.

Joel looked up. "Do they have sisters too?"

Mom replied, "Oh, yes. Mary is seventeen, I think. And Pollyanna and Peter are twenty."

Joel's brow wrinkled. "Pollyanna and Peter? Are they twins?"

"Yes, indeed," laughed Mom.

Joel finished reading the letter.

We got lots of strawberries this year.
Yours truly,
Allan Detweiler

Joel handed the letter to Mom and returned to his row of peas. Mom began picking a row near Joel.

63

"Allan didn't write a word about your apology, did he?" she said quietly.

Joel shook his head. "I guess he forgot all about it."

"Maybe he did. He has probably forgiven you, anyway," said Mom.

That reminded Joel of what Mom had said to Elam a few minutes ago: *An apology isn't real unless we mean it.* Thoughtfully, Joel popped open a pod and scooped the fat peas into his mouth. Had his own apology to Allan been real? Had he really meant it when he said "I'm sorry" in his letter?

Mom was talking again. "There's something more important than the question of whether Allan has forgiven you, though. And that is—have you forgiven Allan?"

Joel was puzzled. "Me—forgive Allan? He didn't do anything to me."

"Well, he didn't actually hurt you by hitting you. But you were hurt by the way he acted towards you," Mom explained. "I hope you have forgiven him and aren't holding a grudge. Holding a grudge is like walking around with a heavy load on your shoulders all the time."

Joel thought that over. He wasn't sure why a grudge was like a heavy load. But the more he thought about it, the more he realized he still had a bad feeling toward Allan. And he also knew it didn't make him happy to feel that way.

"Forgiving someone is like unloading that heavy burden," Mom continued.

Joel nodded. He knew he didn't want to go around lugging a big load. The best thing he could do would be to get rid of that grudge.

64

13. Storm

The Stutzmans were eating dinner on Saturday noon when a knock sounded on the door. Mom rose swiftly and opened it. "Oh, hello, Dan. You're just in time for dinner."

Seventeen-year-old Dan Yoder shook his head smilingly. "Fact is, I've had mine. We had an early dinner so we could start sooner on the hay that's ready." He coughed. "Dad sent me to ask whether one of your boys could help drive the horse for the hayfork. Lizzie and Dorcas get tired of doing it all afternoon."

Joel almost jumped from his chair. He wanted to shout, "Mom, may I go?" But he didn't say it. He knew Elam would be better help than he.

Mom looked at her two eager boys, then back at Dan. "Will Joel do? Elam and I should keep picking peas."

"Sure, Joel will do fine. He's almost as old as Lizzie, isn't he?" came Dan's answer.

Now Joel did leap to his feet. "Do you want me right away?"

"You have time to finish eating," Dan chuckled. "The girls can drive Frammy till you come."

Dan left, and Joel settled down again. But it didn't take him long to wolf down his piece of strawberry shortcake. As soon as Mom let him, he was off across the field to Harveys.

The first load of hay was just coming in from the field when Joel arrived. He watched as the Yoders' black team strained into the harness to pull the bulging load of loose hay up the embankment. Up near the barn door, the team stopped. Instantly Paul set the hayfork. Its big steel jaws grabbed a mouthful of hay. Now it was time for Frammy to go into action! Frammy had once been part of a team, but the other horse had died of old age. Frammy herself was sixteen, but she was still quite capable of pulling the hayfork.

"Shall I take her down the first couple of times?" Lizzie asked.

Joel nodded. He needed to watch a little to be sure how it was done.

"Giddap, Frammy," Lizzie said importantly, tightening her grip on the reins.

Frammy knew exactly what to do. Her big feet went clop, clop, clop down the embankment. She was hitched to a rope stretching through a pulley under the peak of roof, then down to the hayfork. As she went downhill, the hayfork rose and slid along a track right to the haymow. When Frammy stopped, the fork was tripped, dumping its load. Harvey and Vernon were in the mow, ready to fork and tramp the hay into place.

Meanwhile, Lizzie and Frammy clopped back up the hill; the fork returned to the wagon; and Paul reset the fork. Then it was time to repeat the whole process!

It looked easy, and it was, because Frammy was an old pro at it. Soon Joel was taking her reins with just as much confidence as Lizzie.

But after awhile it grew tiresome. There was

66

never much time to rest, because the Yoders had two teams going in the field. As soon as an empty wagon left, a full one took its place. Up and down, up and down went Frammy. Up and down, up and down went Joel. He was glad to change off with Lizzie every now and then.

The weather was muggy and very warm. Sweat poured down Joel's face. It seemed he could never get enough to drink. Dorcas and Ruth were kept busy refilling the water pail! Once they brought cold mint tea. That was even more refreshing than water.

"Looks as if we might get a thunderstorm," Lizzie remarked, pointing to the southwest.

Joel looked at the sky. Huge purple clouds were billowing up. "At least it will cool off then," he remarked. "Giddap, Frammy."

The wind began rising. At first it tugged playfully at loose wisps of hay. But soon gusts rocked the load of hay Joe was bringing in from the field.

Joel clung to his straw hat. "This is going to be a storm!" he shouted above the roar of the wind.

Harvey stuck his head out of the mow. "Better drive that load right in here. We can't unload in this wind, anyhow, and it will probably start raining any minute," he called down to Joe.

Joe guided his team into the upper part of the barn. Then he hurried out to Joel and Lizzie. "Here, I'll unhitch Frammy. You two had better run for the house."

"What about Dan and Paul?" Lizzie asked anxiously. She had to shout to make herself heard.

As he led Frammy away, Joe looked over his shoulder towards the field. "I think they're coming in."

And so they were, even though there was only a little hay on the wagon. The hayloader rattled and bounced along behind.

Joel felt the first big drops of rain splattering against his back. He and Lizzie sprinted to the house. The wind pushed so hard Joel imagined if he flapped his arms he would fly away!

Lizzie's mom smiled as the two children came panting indoors. "It's getting rough out there, isn't it?"

Joel watched out the window as the Yoder men hurried to unhitch the teams and lead them to the stable. The rain came down harder and harder. Soon there was a stamping of feet as the men arrived, breathless, on the porch.

"Soaked to the skin!" declared Vernon, tugging at his wet shirt.

"It's like running through a wall of water," Dan commented.

Lightning flashed. The rumble of thunder blended with the roar of rain. Dad Yoder stood quietly by the window watching the storm. Joel went over to stand near the stove. He shivered a little as he thought of Mom and Elam alone at home.

After awhile Harvey suggested, "How about an early supper, Mom? We can eat while it rains like this, but we can't very well get the cows. Looks like the rain might keep on for awhile yet."

Elsie agreed, "Yes, we'd better have supper. That way chores won't be so late. After all, it's Saturday evening." She bustled about, preparing soup for supper. Lizzie and Dorcas set the table.

"Guess I should be going home," Joel said uncomfortably.

"Not in this rain," Paul told him with a chuckle.

"Your mom and Elam can get along without you for one meal, can't they?" Dan teased.

"Of course," mumbled Joel. In a way he wished he were at home. Yet in spite of the storm, he felt safe and secure in this kitchen, almost safer than during thunderstorms at home. Joel guessed this was because of Dad Yoder. There was something about a dad calmly taking his place at the head of the table that made you feel safe.

The rain was still pouring down when supper was over. Dad Yoder reached for the Bible. "Maybe by the time we've had devotions the rain will let up."

Joel felt warm and happy as he listened to Harvey Yoder's deep voice read the Scripture and lead in prayer. He almost forgot about the storm.

When they all rose from their knees, little Amos exclaimed, "It's morning again!"

Everyone laughed. The three-year-old was right in a way. The kitchen was no longer so gloomy. Toward the northeast the rain clouds could be seen scurrying away.

"The rain has almost stopped," announced Joe, reaching for his hat.

Joel got his hat too. "I better go." He headed for the door, then remembered. "Thanks for supper."

"You're very welcome," Elsie assured him.

Joel decided to follow the road. That field looked pretty wet! Windrowed hay was scattered every which way. Mud squished between Joel's bare toes as he hurried along beside the road. He was glad to be going home to Mom. But he had enjoyed eating supper with the Yoder family. He whispered to himself as he turned in the Stutzman lane, "That's what it would be like if we had a daddy."

14. Flood

The storm was by no means over. Less than an hour after Joel got home, more clouds came boiling up from the horizon. Soon the rain was falling in sheets again.

"Harvey's hay is really getting soaked," observed Joel. He was sitting on the wood box, watching Mom and Elam eat their supper.

A loud rumble of thunder filled the kitchen, startling them. "That sounded real close," Mom said. She went to the window, and after a moment, sat down again. Joel could see she was nervous.

He thought back to supper at the Yoder home. No one had seemed nervous. Joel thought to himself, *Mom probably wouldn't be nervous either if we had a daddy.*

The heavy shower lasted half an hour. When finally the thunder growled away into the distance, the sun was just about setting. It shone with a reddish glow from a band of clear sky appearing on the western horizon.

"I wonder how the creek looks, after all this rain!" Elam exclaimed.

Joel turned to Mom. "May we go out and have a look before we take our baths?"

"Yes, you may, but be back soon. And stay out of the water! The current will be strong," Mom advised.

The boys dashed out to the pasture. "Lady's not here!" exclaimed Joel.

Elam laughed. "Don't worry. I took her indoors when I saw the storm coming."

"Good," said Joel. He peered down the hill to the creek. "Just look at the water! It's spread way up over the field!"

Elam was staring, wide-eyed. "Oh, my! I've never seen it this high before. Hey—what about that cottage in the Stanfields' flats? It must be partly under water." Elam began to run across the field to the fence that formed the property line between the Stutzmans and the Stanfields.

When Joel reached the fence, Elam was pointing and shouting, "Look at that! The cottage is halfway under water."

"Was somebody living there?" Joel asked anxiously.

Elam shook his head. "I doubt it. Sometimes the Stanfields let visitors sleep in the cottage. But nobody would have been asleep at this time of the day."

"They must have furniture and beds in the cottage then. The beds will be ruined," said Joel.

Elam shrugged. "Not much we can do about it. I wouldn't venture into this flood just to rescue a bed."

"Neither would I," agreed Joel. They stood for a few minutes longer, watching the water swirl and eddy near the roof of the cottage. Then they turned back toward the house.

The next day after church, everyone was talking about the storm. The storm in their area had actually been mild. A hurricane had gone through some of the southern states and Central America. Flooding and high winds had caused a lot of damage.

On the way home, Elam said, "Edwin says some of our boys might be going to Central America to help clean up after the flood."

"That's good," commented Mom. "They will surely need help."

"I wish I could go too," Elam said wistfully.

Mom patted his arm. "I imagine that will be work for grown men and boys. But you know—if some of Harvey's boys go, you may be needed to help with their hay."

Joel had another idea. "And maybe we could help John Stanfield clean up his cottage."

"Say, that would be something!" exclaimed Elam.

"Don't forget it's Sunday," Mom reminded them with a chuckle. "No cleaning up today."

They didn't do any cleaning up that evening, but they did go down to the pasture for another look at their own little flood.

"The water is going down fast," observed Joel. "See, the cottage is practically above water again."

Elam marveled, "Look at all the mud! Layers of it, everywhere! Do you think there is mud inside the cottage too?"

"Probably. What a mess that will be!" responded Joel.

The Stanfields' cottage was the first thing the boys thought of Monday morning. "Should we go over and offer to help clean up?" Elam wondered at breakfast. "John and his wife are pretty old for that kind of work."

"Well, the peas are letting up," Mom considered.

"There won't be much picking today. Besides, it is almost too muddy to work in the garden. You may go and offer to help."

Soon after breakfast they were off. Joel lagged a few feet behind Elam as they went up the Stanfields' walk. He was glad to let his older brother do the talking.

Greta Stanfield opened the door when Elam knocked. She was a snowy-haired, wrinkle-cheeked lady of about seventy. "Hello. You're Mary's boys, aren't you?"

"Yes. We saw that your cottage was flooded and thought we would offer to help clean it up," Elam said quickly.

"My, that's nice of you," beamed Greta. "Our son phoned and offered to come up on Saturday to help. But it would be nice to start sooner. Wait, I'll ask John." She hurried off toward the barn, then stopped and looked back. "Come along if you like."

Joel and Elam followed her. The Stanfields' barn was small—really only a hobby barn for the few cattle they kept.

Suddenly Greta put a finger to her lips. "Sh-h-h. I see John is milking the goat. We better keep quiet till he's done. Nanny is new, and she's awfully skittish yet."

Elam and Joel looked at one another. They hadn't known the Stanfields kept a goat. This was interesting!

By peering over a partition they could see John, as snowy-haired as his wife. On a little platform in front of him stood the goat. Nanny kept glancing around nervously while John milked her.

"There. All done," John said. Nanny was off the

73

platform in a single leap.

The elderly man looked up in surprise. "I see we have visitors."

"Yes. These boys came to offer their help in cleaning up the cottage," Greta said in a pleased voice.

"Sounds good," said John with a smile. He handed the pail of goat's milk to Greta. "I was just going down there myself to have a look at the damage. I'll be glad to have you along."

Even though he was nearly seventy, John's strides were energetic. The boys had to hurry to keep up with him as he led the way down to the cottage.

The door hung crazily from one hinge. "Current must have been pretty strong, to do that," John commented. His boots squished in mud as he stepped inside.

Mud was everywhere. It was caked on the chairs, on the table, on the cupboard, on the windowsills, and several inches deep on the floor.

"See that?" asked John, pointing to a dirty line part way up the wall. "That shows how high the water went." He stood there, shaking his head. "This is a real mess. A real mess!"

Elam and Joel stood nearby without saying anything. They felt sorry for their elderly neighbor.

But John wasted no time feeling sorry for himself. He turned to the boys and said with a chuckle, "What are we waiting for? I'm going up to get some shovels."

15. Cleanup

Cleaning up the cottage proved to be hard work. First they had to move furniture outdoors. John's bad back didn't allow him to do heavy lifting, so he mostly gave instructions while the boys did the work.

"I'm afraid these mattresses are ruined," John said shaking his head. "We'll drag them outside, and when my son comes on Saturday, we'll haul them to the dump." Elam and Joel tugged and pulled until they had three soggy twin mattresses lying on the hillside.

Next John examined the couch. It was just as soggy as the mattresses. "Another write-off, I guess. Do you think you can get this out too?"

"It's no heavier than the mattresses," Elam replied, grabbing one end.

When they had it outdoors, Joel stood for a moment, looking at it. "This couch might be all right again after it's dried out," he said hopefully.

Elam wrinkled his nose. "I doubt it. Even if it ever got dry, it would probably be smelly."

"I didn't mean for using in a house," Joel hastened to say.

"What then?"

Joel turned back to the cottage. "Oh, just something." He had an idea, but he didn't want to tell Elam. Not yet.

"Now if we could get the table and chairs outside too, we'd have more room to start cleaning up," John suggested.

By the time all the movable furniture was outdoors, Joel felt as though he were covered with mud! Now the work began in earnest. He and Elam each had a pail and shovel. They scooped up mud from the floor and filled their pails. Then they carried the mud to the creek bank and dumped it.

John helped a little with the shoveling, but he soon stopped, explaining, "My wife—and my doctor—would get really anxious if they saw me doing this. Please don't feel you have to keep at it all morning, boys. Quit before you're totally exhausted."

The boys kept at it even though they were tired. Towards noon John said, "I hope you can stay for lunch. Greta will be happy to fix something."

"We promised Mom we'd be home for dinner," Elam answered. There was a note of regret in his voice. It would have been interesting to have lunch with the Stanfields.

"Shall we come back this afternoon?" Elam offered as he and Joel prepared to leave.

John's eyes twinkled as they ran over the boys' muddy clothes. "I've a feeling your mom will insist on a bath and clean clothes even before you eat. It would be too bad to come back and get dirty right away again. But if you really want to, we could tackle the mess again tomorrow."

"Okay," Elam agreed readily. "The hay won't be ready yet tomorrow."

John had guessed right. Mom had already filled the tub with warm water when the boys got home!

The first thing Joel noticed when they got back to the cottage next morning was the smell. "Phew!" he said, holding his nose. "It didn't smell this bad yesterday, did it?"

Elam shook his head. "Reminds me of a garbage dump."

Just then John Stanfield appeared at the door. "That's a good description," he chuckled.

"Do you think we can get it to smell clean again?" Joel wondered.

John responded, "I hope so. You know, I'm glad we're starting the cleanup before my son Trevor comes. He's a real city boy by this time, even though he grew up on the farm. I have a feeling if he saw— and smelled—the cottage today, he would want to bulldoze it down rather than clean it up."

Elam and Joel grinned at one another and set to work. By eleven o'clock they had scraped up all the mud from the four little rooms.

"Ready for a bath again?" John asked as they left.

"Sure thing," replied Elam. "Do you need help again tomorrow? Mom says there are beans to pick this afternoon."

"Well, if we could get started with hot water and soap, washing walls and things . . ." John said hopefully.

"We'll come if Mom lets us," Elam assured him.

Tramping up the hill, Joel exclaimed, "My, it's good to get some fresh air! That smell is getting worse than a pig barn."

Elam looked at him. "Imagine how much worse the smell will be down in Central America, where whole cities were flooded."

"Paul and Joe Yoder will have some stories to tell when they get back, I guess," said Joel. "Do you think the vanload of boys has reached the disaster area already?"

"I doubt it. They only started off last evening. By the time they get there, the smell will be even worse because of the hot sun and all!"

Joel thought that over. "And I don't suppose the workers down there get the chance to take a bath at noon the way we do."

Elam shook his head. "They will have to keep on all day, I'm sure. I just hope they can take a bath before they go to bed."

On Wednesday morning, John's pickup truck stood near the cottage when the boys arrived. "Hot water!" said the old man with a smile, touching the barrel on the back of the truck. "Gallons and gallons of hot water is what we need today. See, this barrel has a spigot at the bottom. Fill your bucket with hot water, add this soap, and you're ready to start at the high-water mark."

Joel grinned. He liked his elderly neighbor's breezy manner. Soon he and Elam were scrubbing a wall. Elam could reach as high as the dirty water had gone, but Joel had to stand on a stool.

"Whew! The water gets dirty real fast," Joel exclaimed after a few minutes.

"That's why I brought a whole barrel full," John said. "Be sure to use it all up. As soon as the water in your bucket turns dark, get some more."

It seemed to Joel that he spent more time filling and emptying buckets than actually scrubbing. But by noon they had cleaned up several walls. John was pleased with their progress. "I'm going to pay you well," he promised.

"Pay?" asked Elam in surprise as he emptied his final bucket.

"Yes, indeed. You will need pay for such dirty work," John insisted.

Elam shrugged. "We hadn't been thinking about pay. . . . Well, I'll ask my mother."

The boys spent every morning that week at the cottage. Both haymaking and beanpicking were best done in the afternoons anyway. By Friday noon they were still not finished, but the cottage definitely looked better.

"Trevor and I can finish up tomorrow," John said with satisfaction. He reached into his pocket. "And now for your pay."

Elam protested, "This was volunteer work, just like the boys who went down to Central America to help clean up. Mom said we don't need pay."

John smiled. "All right, I won't pay you then. I'll just give each of you a gift." And he pressed a twenty-dollar bill into each boy's hand.

Joel's eyes widened. Twenty dollars! He'd never had so much money in his life. He looked at Elam to see what he would do.

Elam hesitated. "Well, okay. Thanks a lot. We enjoyed working for you."

"Yes, thank you very much," Joel said shyly.

"And thank you, very much!" John responded heartily. He waved as the boys set off up the hill.

"What do you think Mom will say?" Joel asked, gazing at his twenty-dollar bill.

"I don't know," Elam replied. "She said we don't need pay."

Joel ran into the kitchen. "Mom, John didn't pay us, but he gave us each a gift!" He waved the twenty-dollar bill under her nose.

Mom blinked. "Twenty dollars—each!"

"He insisted," Elam said quickly. "He wouldn't take no for an answer."

"I see," said Mom. "Well, I guess you couldn't very well refuse."

Joel felt relieved. He had been afraid Mom would make them take the money back. "What are we going to do with it?" he asked.

"H-m-m-m. It's your money. You earned it," Mom answered.

"I don't even know what to do with so much money," Elam declared.

"Shall I put it in a safe place for now? We could all think it over for a day or two," Mom suggested.

16. A Noble Thing

Joel was eating his egg the next morning when he remembered. "That couch!" he said suddenly. Then he coughed and spluttered because something got stuck in his windpipe.

Mom patted his back. "What did you say, anyway? Something about a couch?"

"Yes," said Joel sheepishly. "John had a little couch in the cottage that got all wet. He said Trevor would haul it to the dump today. But I just thought. . . ." He hesitated. He wasn't sure what Mom and Elam would think of his plan.

"You thought what?" prompted Elam.

"Well, that couch was drying in the sun all week, and it doesn't smell too bad. I sniffed it again yesterday, to make sure." Joel paused again, looking first at Mom then at Elam. Then he plunged on, "I thought—if John still doesn't want it—that couch would be nice for our cave."

At first Elam looked surprised. Then he started laughing. "Good idea, Joel! Then if Allan Detweiler ever comes again, he won't need to get his good pants dirty sitting on the floor!"

"That's not why I thought of it," Joel said crossly. Was Elam making fun of his plan?

"If we want that couch, we'll have to rescue it before Trevor Stanfield comes," Elam said briskly.

Joel smiled happily and asked Mom, "May we go

down again this morning? We'll be back soon to help weed the garden."

"All right," Mom agreed. "If it doesn't take long. We do have a lot of work today, and Elam will be helping Harvey with the hay again this afternoon."

"Have you thought what you'll do with your money?" Elam asked as they headed for the cottage.

"I've thought about it, but that's all," Joel admitted. "What about you?"

"Well, the other day Mom was talking again about buying Will. She'd really like to."

"I don't see why," Joel interrupted.

"I do. Will's a fairly dependable horse, even if he is slow. Anyway," Elam went on, "Mom said she would rather not use any of our savings to buy Will, because it's good to have a little money for emergencies. But she doesn't have quite enough money in the checking account to buy Will, even though he is a real cheap horse. Maybe our forty dollars would help."

"Don't talk about 'our forty dollars.' I haven't decided about my twenty yet," Joel replied sharply.

"Okay, okay," Elam said in a way that Joel found very irritating.

John's pickup truck was already parked at the cottage. A tall, broad shouldered man was struggling to pull the mattresses onto the back. "Hi, I'm Trevor," he called. "Are you the kind fellows who were helping Dad all week?"

Elam nodded, feeling shy with this stranger from the city.

"Looks like I could use a little more help, getting these mattresses and couch onto the truck," Trevor admitted.

Elam sprang over to help. Joel watched anxiously. Was Elam going to say something about the couch? As Trevor reached for the couch, Elam asked hesitantly, "Could we have that, since you don't want it?"

"Why, sure," Trevor said with a hint of surprise. "Shall I drive the couch up to your house?"

"As a matter of fact," Elam said sheepishly, "we'd like to have it down by the creek. We have a little cave . . ."

Trevor laughed, "Aha, a hideout. Here, we'll load up the couch and drive it right to the creek bank. Maybe you'll let me see your cave in return."

"Of course," Elam said readily.

A few minutes later, they were at the creek. As they tugged the couch off the truck, Trevor asked, "You mean the cave is on Dad's land? I never knew there was one when I was a boy."

"Maybe it wasn't here then. It's just a hollow place under this big cedar tree," Elam explained.

Trevor helped lug the couch down the bank, then peered into the cave. It smelled dank because it had been flooded too. "This is a splendid hideout," he declared. Then he added with a grin, "And now that you have a couch, it'll be even more splendid."

After Trevor's truck had roared off up the hill, the boys sat for a few minutes on their "splendid" couch. Soon Elam sprang up exclaiming, "We'd better go back home."

Joel got up reluctantly. "Let's follow the creek to our property and go up through our pasture."

"Okay," agreed Elam, starting off at a fast trot. Soon they came to the line fence which ran right through the creek to keep in the Stutzman's horses.

Joel vaulted over the fence—and then stopped short. "What's that?"

Elam looked where Joel was pointing. Something gray was moving around in the rushes at the water's edge. Elam stared for a moment, then burst out laughing. "Why, it's Nanny, John's goat!"

"So it is," exclaimed Joel. "But what does she want on our land? I thought John fenced off the upper part of his pasture for her."

Elam sniffed. "Goats are smarter than fences. A lot smarter! They don't need a very big hole to get through. Come on, let's chase her back home before she finds her way to our garden!"

"She couldn't get into our garden, could she?" Joel protested.

"If she can get out of her own pasture, she can find a way through any fence on our property," Elam declared. "Let's circle quietly behind her."

Nanny looked up as the boys approached. "Maa-a-a," she bleated mischievously, skipping up the hill. Soon she slipped through a hole in the fence, back into her own pasture.

"That was easy," panted Joel.

Elam was the first to reach Mom in the garden. "Sorry we're late. We had to chase Nanny around first."

"Nanny? Oh, you mean the Stanfields' goat! Isn't the fence tight?" asked Mom.

"Afraid not," replied Elam as he began hoeing weeds.

"Then we'll have to do something about it— today!" declared Mom.

Joel protested, "Why we? It's not our goat."

Mom looked at him. "I gather the hole is in the

upper part of the line fence?"

"Yes."

"The upper half is ours to maintain," Mom said firmly.

"But the fence is good enough for horses, even if it isn't good enough for a goat. Trevor and his dad could fix it today," Joel grumbled.

"Joel," said Mom, "it must be time for another lesson in willingness. Think of the way you worked all week to clean up that smelly cottage. That was hard, dirty work, wasn't it? Yet you did it willingly, didn't you?"

Joel nodded uncomfortably.

Mom went on with a hint of a smile, "We humans are like that. If we think of a project ourselves, we can slave away willingly for hours—especially if it seems like a noble thing to do. But as soon as we're asked to do something we think somebody else ought to do—then it's a different story!"

Joel had to smile too. It really was silly, when he thought about it.

"We ought to be willing to do whatever needs to be done, even when it doesn't seem at all like a noble thing," Mom said quietly.

17. A Sudden Trip

Mom stayed out hoeing weeds until nearly twelve noon that Saturday. Then she hustled toward the house, calling over her shoulder to the boys, "I'll have dinner ready in ten minutes!"

"We must be having canned vegetable soup if she can have dinner ready in ten minutes," Joel remarked.

"That's good. I like vegetable soup," Elam responded.

Joel sniffed. There were things he liked better than vegetable soup. Sure enough, a few minutes later, they were greeted by the familiar aroma of vegetable soup. Joel knew better than to complain.

They had barely started eating when there was a knock on the door. It was Solomon Raber who lived on the next farm beyond the Yoders. Solomon ran a hand through his sandy hair. "I don't suppose you'd be interested in going away over the weekend?"

"This weekend?" Mom asked in a startled voice.

Solomon chuckled. "Well, yes. We and the Millers had hired a van to take us to Lavender County. But the Millers let us know an hour ago that they can't go because their baby is sick. So we asked my brother Edward to go along, but they have only two children, so the van is still not full. There is room for you and the boys, if you'd like."

Lavender County! Joel almost jumped from his

chair. That was where both sets of their grandparents lived. He wanted to shout, "Let's go, Mom!" But because Solomon was there, he only looked at her with pleading eyes.

"You would be starting off tonight? What time?" Mom asked slowly.

Joel and Elam cast eager glances at one another. This sounded promising!

"Six-thirty. It takes about an hour and a half to get there, wouldn't you say?"

Mom smiled at the boys' eager faces. "What do you think? Shall we surprise Grandpa Kings tonight?"

Both boys grinned widely and nodded vigorously.

Mom turned to Solomon again. "Would we be staying for supper tomorrow?"

"That's the plan," answered the young man.

"Then we could have supper at Grandpa Stutzmans," Mom said with satisfaction. "Yes, we'll go. Thanks for asking us."

Solomon flashed a smile and turned to go. "I better hurry, or I won't get everything done that I should before we leave," he said.

"That goes for us too," Mom said. "Boys, I'm afraid we won't get the whole garden weeded. There are still some beans to pick. . . ."

"And that fence to fix," Elam reminded her.

"Oh, yes. Well, we'll do that first. I'll come with you and have a look. Get the hammer and pliers and some big staples. We may need some wire too," Mom directed.

Elam found a roll of wire and hefted it to his shoulder. Joel carried the tools and staples. Mom was already heading down to the pasture. They followed her at a fast trot.

"Was this the place?" asked Mom, pointing to a spot where the bottom wire was broken.

"I think so," Elam replied.

Mom examined the fence for a few minutes, then suggested how to fix it. "Think you can do it?" she asked Elam. "I better get back to the garden. A customer is coming at three."

"We'll do something about it," Elam promised. He began removing some wire from the roll. "Here, Joel, hang on to this end."

They worked for half an hour, stretching the wire and pounding staples into the posts. Joel kept glancing over at the Stanfields' buildings. "No sign of anybody over there. Think they have all gone away?"

Elam was too busy to do anything but shrug. Joel continued grumbling, "They won't even find out we had to fix the fence for their goat."

"Why would they have to?" Elam asked shortly.

"Well, they could at least know what a nuisance that goat is. And I still think they should have made sure the fence is tight before letting her out," Joel declared.

Elam stared at him for a moment with raised eyebrows. Then he turned wordlessly back to his repairs. Joel decided he'd better be quiet too.

The afternoon fled by on wings. After the fence was done, the boys helped Mom with the beans. Then they hoed weeds as fast as they could until it was time to get ready for their journey.

"Let's walk out the lane, then the van won't have to drive in," Mom suggested as she tied her bonnet. The boys were so excited that they found it hard to walk—so they ran instead.

When Mom joined them near the mailbox, the van was still nowhere in sight. Joel began to fidget. "If we're late, Grandpa Kings will be in bed when we get there."

Elam pulled out his watch. "It's only six-forty. Oh, there he comes!"

"Hi, boys," greeted Norm, the van-driver, as they climbed in through the sliding door. "So you're going to your grandparents!"

Joel nodded. This wasn't the first time they were going with Norm to Lavender County.

Darkness fell as the van sped along. After awhile the road dipped downward. Spread in the valley below them was a sea of lights. "That's the town of Lionel," Elam informed Joel.

"Lionel? That's not far from Grandpas, is it?" Joel asked excitedly.

"They're about six miles on the other side of Lionel," Elam guessed.

The van slowed along the main street. Joel stared in fascination at the blinking neon lights on the storefronts.

Soon they left the town behind, and in only a short time Norm turned in a driveway. "Is this Grandpas?" Joel whispered.

"Don't you know?" Elam asked.

Joel pushed his nose against the window. "I can't see. It's too dark."

"Well, this is Uncle Aarons' house—remember? And the little part at the back belongs to Grandpas," Elam said importantly.

Mom and the boys left the van and walked up Grandpas' walk. Lamplight shone from their kitchen window. When Mom knocked, the door opened, and there stood Grandpa King. At first he looked surprised, and then very pleased. "Mary! And the boys. You've come for the night, I'm sure?"

Instantly Grandma was at the door too. Joel always thought she looked like Mom, only older. Soon all of them were seated around the table, the boys mostly listening while the grown-ups talked and talked. Mom and her mother wrote regularly to each other, but it seemed they always had lots left over to say when they met!

All too soon it was time for bed. "Can you sleep in the storeroom again, boys?" Grandma asked with a twinkle in her eyes.

Joel nodded, remembering the last time they had slept here. They trooped upstairs with Grandma and helped her lay a piece of foam rubber on the storeroom floor. There was just barely room among the boxes and odds and ends. Then Grandma brought some bedding, and it was time to turn in.

Joel couldn't sleep right away. The hard floor had a way of making itself felt through the foam rubber. The room had a grandmotherly smell to it—dried tea leaves and old clothes. Joel had fond memories of being allowed to play in here sometimes, peeking into boxes and discovering treasures.

When he fell asleep, Joel dreamed of opening the big trunk in the corner and watching a goat jump out.

18. A New Fence

On Monday morning the boys slept late. Sunlight was streaming in Joel's window when he opened his eyes. He yawned and stretched lazily. Memories of the trip to Lavender County floated through his head: breakfast at Grandpa Kings; walking a mile and a half to the farm where church was held; the many people at church, all strangers except for his cousins. Then supper at Grandpa Stutzmans, and a marvelous game of hide-and-seek with their cousins who lived on the same farm, until Norm came and brought them home again.

"Joel! Elam! Breakfast," Mom called up the stairs. Joel sprang into action and managed to beat Elam downstairs. The kitchen was filled with the aroma of toast and fried eggs. Joel had a hard time remembering not to speak with his mouth full that morning. There were so many things to talk about.

They were nearly done eating when Elam said, "Mom, I've decided you can have my twenty dollars to use for buying Will if you need it."

Mom smiled appreciatively. "That would help out." She paused. "Grandpa Stutzman was telling me something last night that might interest you too. A fund is being set up to help disaster victims in Central America. Anyone who wants to contribute can give a donation to the deacon in his district."

Elam looked thoughtful. "You're suggesting those

91

twenty dollars should go there?"

"I don't know," Mom admitted. "It's true more money is needed if I want to buy Will without breaking into our savings."

"I guess we could give ten dollars to the fund and keep ten for Will," Elam said.

Mom nodded. "That might be the way to do it."

All this time, Joel was listening uncomfortably. Was Mom going to ask about his twenty dollars? He wasn't ready to give it up the way Elam was planning to.

A knock sounded on the door. This time it was Vernon Yoder. "I guess you're wondering what happened to your garden while you were gone," he said, without taking time to say hello.

"Our garden? What do you mean?" Mother asked in a puzzled voice.

"So you haven't been out since you're home. I'm afraid it's a bit messed up," Vernon said apologetically.

"Messed up?" Mom got to her feet and went to the window. The boys joined her. Joel couldn't see anything the matter. There were the bean rows, and the bare patch where the peas had been.

"Some tomatoes got squashed," Vernon was saying. "That goat of Stanfields was in your garden when we came over to do chores last night. We tried to get her out quickly, but she led us on a wild goose chase first."

"Oh-h-h," Mom's voice was strained. "I thought we fixed the fence . . ."

"Shall we help?" Vernon offered.

Mom thought for a moment. "We'll take a look at it ourselves first. If we need any help, we'll let you know. Thanks."

There was a little smile on Elam's face. He was pleased Mom was giving him the chance to repair the fence himself.

But none of them felt very pleased when they went out to inspect the garden. The tomato plants were severely damaged. Sharp little hoofprints were everywhere.

"It looks like Nanny tried as hard as she could to step on every tomato in sight," muttered Elam.

Mom stooped to pick up a smashed tomato. "Just when they were turning ripe . . ." she mourned.

"She was in the cucumber patch too," Joel called. He held up a big cucumber with its insides oozing out.

"Are there any nice ones left? I've a customer coming for some big ones today," said Mom.

Joel hunted among the prickly vines. "Yes, some are still all right."

Mom's lips formed a tight line. "We'll fix that fence first thing this morning." She hurried towards the pasture while the boys went after the hammer and staples.

"See this?" Mom asked when they came down to the fence. "The bottom wire is bent up in three different places. That goat simply burrows through!"

"I guess the fence is pretty old if it bends that easily," Elam observed.

"H-m-m-m," said Mom. "Can we afford to replace this whole stretch of fence? If we do, then we needn't wonder what to do with your twenty dollars!" She looked at Elam.

Joel protested, "That wouldn't be fair. It's Stanfields' goat—not ours!"

Mom leveled a look at him. "It's our fence."

Joel was seething. He watched as Elam got down on his hands and knees for a closer look at the damage.

"Joel, did you hear when the minister spoke about going the second mile yesterday?" Mom asked.

Joel squirmed. "Yes," he admitted.

Mom went on, "He reminded us that Jesus went further even than the second mile. He went the fourth and the fifth mile too, when He died for our sins. So if He is our example, we should be ready to do more than we're obligated to do . . . even if it doesn't seem fair."

Elam scrambled to his feet. "Maybe if we'd stretch a new wire all along the bottom, that would keep the goat in."

"It might," Mom said doubtfully.

"There comes John Stanfield!" Joel said excitedly, pointing to the stooped figure walking across the pasture.

Mom looked up. "We'll see what he has to say."

"Anything the matter?" John asked brightly as he approached.

Joel felt like saying, *Yes, indeed, there is something the matter.* But of course he didn't say it. He waited to see how Mom would react.

"We're just discovering that our fence needs repairs," Mom replied pleasantly.

"Why? Your horses getting too frisky?"

"Well, no, as a matter of fact, the horses are okay. But your goat seems to like our garden—"

"My goat!" John interrupted in a horrified voice. He began examining the wire. "This fence is too old. Nanny can bend the wires whichever way she pleases."

Joel thought, *Exactly. So now you want us to put up a new fence.* He was feeling belligerent indeed.

"I'm going to phone the Laurentian Fence Company right away. If they can come soon, they'll have a new fence up by tomorrow evening," John said briskly.

Amazed, Joel watched the elderly man hurry away. Then he turned to Mom. "I guess he knows how to go the second mile."

Mom nodded and smiled. Together they walked up through the field. By the time they reached the garden, Joel had made up his mind what to do with his twenty dollars. He had learned a few things about going the second mile too.

19. Thieves

It was time for Lady to get into harness again. Mr. Duval had pronounced her roadworthy, and Elam could hardly wait to hitch her up. "Will we take her to the blacksmith today?" he asked Mom after the vet had gone.

"We have to go through town to get to the blacksmith," Mom said doubtfully. "Lady might be hard to handle after such a long rest."

"Are you afraid Lady will get away from us?" asked Elam.

Mom smiled and shook her head. "No, I don't think so. All right, you may get her harnessed."

The trip to the blacksmith was uneventful. Lady minced along gingerly, as though she didn't quite trust her feet. On the way home she seemed more confident. The reins were taut in Mom's hands as Lady strained to go faster.

"She likes her new shoes," Mom said, gripping the reins more firmly.

Suddenly Lady tossed her head. Disregarding the reins, she flattened out and ran as Joel had never seen her run before. His heart was in his mouth. The buggy careened from side to side.

"Help me, Elam," Mom called above the rattle of the wheels. Her face was white.

Elam reached over and grabbed the reins just in front of Mom's hands. Both of them pulled with all their might, sawing at Lady's mouth. Gradually she slowed, and Joel dared to breathe again.

Elam let go of the reins. "Feeling pretty frisky, I guess," he remarked with a shaky chuckle.

"A far cry from the Willing Jaybird," Mom commented. Her voice was shaky too.

Joel said nothing, but he was thinking, *I guess it's a good thing we bought Will, after all. At least he's safe to drive.*

After dinner that day, the boys went with their mother to the sweetcorn patch. Joel felt the fat ears, waiting to see what Mom would say. She parted the silken leaves and peered into a few of the cobs. "Ready for sale!" she announced. "We should put up the sign right away."

Joel and Elam hurried to the shed and dusted off the "Sweet Corn" sign. After they set it up by the roadside, Elam predicted, "It won't be long till the first car stops. Sweet corn is our best-selling produce."

He was right. By evening Mom had made no less than six trips to the corn patch to serve customers. Most people seemed to like watching their corn being picked directly from the stalks. That way they knew it was fresh!

"Is all the ripe corn gone?" Elam asked Mom that evening.

She shook her head. "I took a quick estimate. There might be another six dozen there for tomorrow. And the next variety of corn is nearly ready too. Let's leave the sign out."

By eight-thirty the next morning, the day's first customer had arrived. Elam and Joel went with

Mom to the patch because Mr. Hillingsworth wanted five dozen. The boys could help carry the ears to his car.

Mom led the way down the rows of corn. Soon Joel heard her exclaim in dismay, "Why, where are the ripe ears I saw yesterday? Am I in the wrong row?"

"Perhaps you are," said Mr. Hillingsworth.

Mom slipped over into the next row. "None here either." She turned and stared wide-eyed at Elam. "Somebody must have helped himself to our corn last night."

"Why not look in this row?" Mr. Hillingsworth suggested.

Mom shook her head. "That's a different variety. Not ready yet." Her face was flushed. "I'm sorry, Mr. Hillingsworth. There is no corn here for you. I hope you realize this wasn't intentional . . ."

"No, I'm sure it wasn't," said Mr. Hillingsworth impatiently. "I was looking forward to some fresh sweet corn. Well, I'll be back in a day or two." He hurried to his car.

Elam's teeth were clenched as he glared after the portly man. "All he cares about is having his corn. He doesn't even care that we have been robbed."

Mom smiled slightly. "No use being angry about that."

But Elam was angry, if not at Mr. Hillingsworth, then at the corn thief. "Who would have done such a thing?" he asked indignantly. "It must have been one of yesterday's customers, because the thief knew exactly where to look. H-m-m-m. Maybe it was the one with the long hair."

Joel was getting excited too. "Or maybe it was

that lady whose face was all painted up. Remember? Even her fingernails were painted."

But Mother rebuked them. "Boys, boys. We don't know who it was, and we probably never shall. We won't waste any time trying to figure it out either. Go bring in the sign."

"The nerve of them," Elam muttered to Joel as they went out to the road to get the sign. "I can't understand why anyone would steal produce from a widow." His voice choked with anger.

Joel was silent. He didn't often see Elam so worked up.

Elam was still fuming that afternoon when Edwin Miller stopped by. It wasn't long until Elam had told him the whole story.

Edwin laughed. "Are you sure it wasn't raccoons? We have trouble with coons and skunks raiding our patch."

Elam shook his head. "I don't think so. Coons usually make a mess of the patch, pulling down stalks, don't they?"

Edwin nodded. "Usually. Can we have a look at your corn patch?"

"Sure. Come on."

Soon Edwin was examining the rows that had been robbed. "H-m-m. It does look like humans, all right. I guess you can't use the same methods to stop them as we did to trick the coons."

"What did you do?" Joel wanted to know.

"We took a bunch of baler twine and strung it up between the stalks. Somebody told us that coons hate to get their feet tangled up in string."

"Did it help?"

Edwin shrugged. "We're getting enough corn for

our own use, anyway."

When Edwin was gone, Elam said thoughtfully, "We could string up some baler twine too. Remember, Harvey bought some baled hay this spring, so there's a pile of twine in our barn."

Joel stared at him. "But why? Edwin said himself it wasn't coons that stole our corn."

Elam was already headed for the barn. "Well, at least we can make sure the coons don't get some too!"

Joel grabbed an armload of twine and followed Elam. He watched to see how Elam did it, stringing up twine in a zig-zag line from stalk to stalk. "You know," said Joel after awhile, "if a real thief were to come in here at night, he'd probably stumble over this twine."

Elam grinned at him. "Maybe I thought of that too."

Joel was surprised and troubled. What would their mother think of this idea?

A day later, Mom said at breakfast, "I'm going out to check the corn. If the next variety is ready, we'll put up the sign again. You boys coming?"

Joel looked at Elam, who shook his head. "No, I guess not." He looked uncomfortable.

When Mom came back, she made a beeline straight to where the boys were pulling weeds in the garden. Her voice was stern. "Elam! Was that twine your idea?"

Elam nodded sheepishly. "I figured we could at least keep the coons out."

Mom said sharply, "But you weren't doing it just for coons."

Elam's eyes met hers, then dropped again. "I

guess not."

"You go and take down that twine right away! We don't want anyone getting hurt in our corn patch— even if it's someone stealing our corn." Mom's voice softened. "And besides, Elam, that is no way to turn the other cheek, is it?"

Elam was still looking at the ground. "I guess not," he said again.

20. Art Project

The summer days passed swiftly. There was no more trouble with thieves in the corn patch. The crop was good, and the Stutzmans sold several hundred dozen ears.

Before long it was time for school to start. Joel was glad, but Elam wasn't too sure. He enjoyed working in the produce patch. Both boys liked their teacher, though. Teacher Helen had been teaching at West Bend for seven years, so neither of them had ever had another teacher.

If Helen Miller enjoyed teaching one subject more than any other, it was art. She was an artist herself and did illustrating for a publishing company.

There were times when Joel wished Teacher Helen didn't like drawing so well, for she expected her pupils to learn it too. Joel was convinced he was not an artist. His horses looked like cows, and his people tended to resemble cornstalks, or even trees.

But even Joel became enthused about the art project his teacher introduced in early October. "How many of you," she asked that Friday, "had brothers who went down to Central America to clean up after the flood?"

Joel was mystified. What could that have to do with art? He glanced around the room. Quite a few hands went up.

"And did your brothers tell you about that

102

orphanage they cleaned up?"

Heads nodded vigorously everywhere. Joel understood because Paul Yoder had talked about it.

"Wasn't that something?" Teacher Helen went on. "Think of those two hundred children having to leave the orphanage the night of the storm! They were moved to a school building in a higher part of the city, and there they tried to sleep on the floor. After the flood, they couldn't move back into the orphanage right away, so they lived in many different places until the building was cleaned up and repaired."

Joel looked across the aisle at Edwin. This was an interesting art period, with the teacher telling stories instead of giving out a drawing assignment!

Teacher Helen's voice softened. "What I really want you to think about is this: What would it be like to live in an orphanage with several hundred children? There would be some adults to care for you, but they wouldn't have time to spend with you the way your parents do. They would probably be rushed off their feet simply to make sure you had clothes and food. The orphanage supervisors might love all those little children—but they would have little time to show it!"

Joel swallowed hard. He had never given much thought to what an orphanage would be like. His teacher made it sound pathetic.

Teacher went on, "Anyway, to make a long story short . . ."

Joel hid a smile. That was her favorite expression. "To make a long story short . . ." she would often say as she set out to explain a difficult math concept.

". . . the board members and I got together, and

we came up with something we could do for the children in that orphanage, something to convey a little touch of love to them this winter." Teacher Helen smiled at the surprised looks on the children's faces. "We are going to make little toys—as many as we can—and put them in a big parcel to mail down."

The whole classroom was electrified. Joel found himself on the edge of his seat, waiting to see what toys they would make.

"We've written the orphanage, you see," Teacher Helen explained, "and they sent us a list of their youngest children's names, from ages four to six. There are sixty of them! We hope to send each child an individually-wrapped package with his or her name on it." She paused. "I can see you are just bursting to see what we will make. Well, I'm hoping you will come up with ideas of your own too. But for starters, I have some simple wood patterns for the boys in Grades 4 to 8. The older girls will make rag dolls and stuffed toys. And all the younger children will make picture books."

Everyone looked at everyone else, nodding and smiling happily. Teacher Helen began organizing things. The older girls were allowed to gather in a corner of the classroom with the patterns and material scraps the teacher provided. Then she got the little ones started cutting out pictures. And finally, she handed the woodworking patterns to the boys. "Since you haven't brought your saws and things, about all you can do today is decide which pattern you will use. When you've done that, you may do catch-up work."

Joel decided on a wooden cat that could wag its tail. The instructions showed it painted bright orange, with black stripes like a tiger. As he walked home from school with Elam, Joel asked, "Do you think Teacher will let us paint or varnish our toys too?"

"I hope so," responded Elam. "I'm going to make a horse and cart. I'd like to paint the cart red."

When they came home, both of them started in at once, telling their mother about their wonderful art project. Mom listened and asked questions patiently until she had the full story. "That sounds like an excellent idea," she said.

That evening after supper Mom announced, "I have some news for you too. I'm going on a trip!"

"You're going on a trip? Without us?" Elam asked in surprise.

"Yes. To Ohio."

Joel was surprised too. Always before, when Mother went somewhere, they had gone along. "How long will you be away?"

"Six days. We start off on Wednesday and come back the following Tuesday," Mom replied.

"Who's going with you?" Elam wondered.

"Sam Millers and Enos Swartzentrubers. We're going by Greyhound."

"I wish I could go along," Joel said glumly.

"I know," said Mom kindly. "It's going to be hard for me to leave you behind. But I'm sure you'll enjoy living at Harveys for a week."

"That should be fun," Elam said enthusiastically.

But Joel was not enthusiastic. He hated the thought of seeing Mom go away.

As it happened, Joel didn't even see her leave. Wednesday morning he and Elam started off for school as usual. That evening they came back to a house that was cold and empty. Picking up the suitcases Mom had packed for them, they went over to Harveys.

"I feel like one of those orphans we're making toys for," Joel said gloomily as they walked in the Yoders' lane.

"Ah, come on!" laughed Elam. "Just because Mom's gone for a few days."

"She'll be gone for a whole week," Joel reminded him.

"Not a whole week," Elam objected, "just six days."

Then it was time to stop quarreling because they had reached Harveys' kitchen door. Mom Yoder greeted them with a big smile. She showed them where they would sleep. Then she said, "The children are all in the barn, playing hide-and-seek."

The hide-and-seek game did wonders for Joel. By supper time he had forgotten about being an orphan. In fact, as the days passed he enjoyed life at Harveys more and more. There was something special about being part of a big family. He liked playing with little Amos and Adam. Even one-year-old Roy could be fun to play with sometimes. And it was nice to pretend that Paul, Joe, Dan and Vernon were really his big brothers. As for Lizzie, Dorcas, and Ruth, they were often good fun too, in spite of being girls.

Tuesday afternoon came around quickly. "Today we go home instead of to Harveys," Elam remarked as he and Joel left school.

"I almost wish Mom would stay away longer," Joel admitted.

Elam turned on him in astonishment. "You—what?"

Joel felt his face grow warm. "Well, what I meant was, I liked being at Harveys."

"So did I," agreed Elam.

But as they neared home, they began to run. Suddenly Joel wanted very much to see Mom! There she was, standing in the kitchen doorway, watching for them. When Joel skidded to a stop at the door, she reached out and gave him a big hug. "Why, I almost forgot how you look!" she exclaimed.

Joel took in his mom's dear face, and her graying hair. "Me, too," he admitted. "I almost forgot how you look too."

When Joel went to bed that night he prayed, "Thank You, God, for letting Mom come safely home again."

21. Appendicitis

By November the "toy box" at the back of the
West Bend classroom was full and overflowing.
There were wooden toys, picture books, and rag
dolls in abundance. "It's time to wrap up our gifts,"
Teacher Helen announced one Friday. She produced
a large roll of plain, brown wrapping paper and
began cutting off pieces. Each child was given paper
and a toy; then Helen gave instructions on how to
wrap it securely.

"Now before you forget what toy you wrapped,
we'll put a child's name on each parcel. Here's the
list they sent us. H-m-m-m. These Spanish names
are quite strange. I see they put 'b' or 'g' beside each
one so we'll know whether it's a boy or a girl. We'll
start with you, Edwin. You have a wooden boat?
Write 'To Juan Cemo.' Esther? A rag doll? Write
'Alicia Seran' . . ." And so on she went, right down
the list. Joel wrapped his own orange-and-black cat.
It was going to a four-year-old boy named José.

Walking home with Elam later, Joel mused, "I
wonder what little José looks like. I wish I could see
his face when he opens that package."

"I think all those little orphans will be surprised
and happy," Elam responded.

"Please let me tell Mom we wrapped the packages today," Joel begged. "You got to tell her about
the Martins' new baby last night."

"Okay," Elam agreed grudgingly. He and Joel often quarreled over who should be the first to tell Mom something.

Mom wasn't in the kitchen. "Mo-om!" Joel called.

"Here. In the bedroom," came her voice. It sounded strangely weak.

Joel sprinted to the bedroom door. "May we come in?"

"Yes."

He went to her bed. Mom was terribly pale.

"I'm sorry," she gasped. "Elam, you will have to . . . call the doctor . . . my stomach hurts so bad . . . I'm almost sure . . . appendicitis . . ." Her words ended in a groan.

"Do you want the doctor to come?" Elam asked, white-faced.

"Probably not. Tell him . . . pain real bad . . . tell what I suspect . . . he'll get ambulance. Tell Harveys too."

Joel was stunned. Ambulance! He sat down near Mom's bed while Elam dashed from the house. All thought of what he had planned to tell Mom had fled. Only very sick people were put in ambulances! "Will . . . will you go to the hospital?" he asked anxiously.

"I'm afraid so," Mom replied weakly. "You liked it at Harveys' when I was in Ohio, didn't you?"

Joel said nothing. Going to Harveys' because Mom was in the hospital would be an entirely different story. He sat mutely near Mom, shivering with dread. Every now and then she moaned softly. Once, she reached over and touched his hand. "I'll probably be away for a day or two. But don't worry, God is always near us."

After what seemed a long time, Elam came back. He sat down on another chair. "The ambulance is on the way. Elsie will be over soon. She says she'll go to the hospital with you."

"Oh, good," Mom whispered.

Minutes later the ambulance screeched in the lane. Two men carried a stretcher indoors. They asked Mom some questions, then put her on the stretcher. Mom Yoder hurried up just before the ambulance was ready to leave. Before climbing in, she said, "Boys, you may go over to our house. Lizzie is making supper tonight."

Never in his life had Joel felt so lost and desolate. He stood watching until the ambulance was out of sight.

Then Elam tugged at his coat sleeve. "Come on. We'll get cold standing here. You heard what Elsie said."

Woodenly, Joel trudged after his older brother out the lane. It was too muddy to go through the fields.

"Lizzie just turned twelve," Elam was saying. "I wonder if she can actually cook supper?"

Joel didn't care. He didn't want supper anyway.

The Yoders' kitchen was warm and noisy. The littlest ones stopped their playing for a few minutes when Joel and Elam arrived. But they couldn't keep still for long, and soon it was noisy again. Joel sat gloomily on the wood box. Every now and then he glanced at Lizzie. She was industriously cutting potatoes and carrots into little chunks and putting them into a pot. Soon the soup was bubbling on the woodstove.

Dorcas and Ruth helped set the table. In spite of himself, Joel grew more and more interested in what the girls were doing. They went about their work so seriously! They looked just like little mothers.

Supper was ready when the men came in. Dad Yoder praised the girls for managing so well. But sixteen-year-old Vernon was not so kind. He took one spoonful of the soup and declared, "This tastes burnt!"

Joel tasted it too. It was true that the soup was not as good as his mom made. But Dad Yoder silenced everybody by saying, "A burnt flavor makes the soup taste just right."

Joel managed to eat some of the first course but refused the pie. Whenever he thought of Mom, off somewhere in the hospital, his stomach went into knots.

After supper Dad Yoder asked, "Do you want to come to the barn, Joel and Elam?"

Joel shrugged. He much preferred to stay in the house so he would be there when Elsie came back. But after Elam decided to go out, Joel did too.

Mom Yoder had not returned by the time they came in again. Joel sat on the wood box once more, watching as Lizzie got the younger children off to bed. Soon Dad Yoder came in from the barn too. Joel was afraid Harvey would make him go to bed, but he didn't. So Joel huddled near the stove, watching the hands of the clock creep past nine o'clock and slowly on towards ten.

At a quarter to ten, Dad Yoder put down his book. He peered at Joel and Elam over the top of his reading glasses. "Would you like to go to bed?"

Joel shook his head. Elam asked, "Is—is Mom Yoder coming back tonight?"

"I think so. But it might be late."

Just then they heard a car motor. Joel sprang to the window. He could dimly make out Elsie Yoder coming up the walk.

Then she came inside, and he held his breath, waiting.

Mom Yoder smiled kindly at the boys. "They operated on your mother soon after we got to the hospital. Her appendix had burst, so it's no wonder she was so sick. But she'll be all right," Mom Yoder added reassuringly. "The doctor said the operation went well."

"When can she come home?" Elam asked in his matter-of-fact way.

Elsie shook her head. "I don't know. It will be a few days at least. But do you know what? I've already asked the man who brought me home tonight, to take us down tomorrow again."

"Us?" croaked Joel. "Can we go to see her?"

"You certainly can. So now, I'm sure, you'll want to go to bed."

Joel nodded. Suddenly he felt very tired. But once under the blankets, he couldn't sleep right away. He kept thinking of Mom, lying alone in a hospital bed far away. How lonely she must be! Then he remembered to pray. "Be near to my mother, Lord Jesus," he prayed. Soon he fell asleep.

Joel hung back. Now that they were actually approaching the door to Mom's hospital room, he felt shy. But Elam was marching right ahead with Elsie Yoder, so Joel couldn't very well stay behind.

He blinked twice as they entered the room. Was that Mom? That pale face on the pillow—was that Mom's?

Then she opened her eyes and smiled. That made her look more like Mom. Joel went up to her, and she reached out to take his hand. "Having an operation makes you pretty sick," she said, her voice barely above a whisper.

Joel stood there, holding his hat. He couldn't think of a single thing to say.

Elam began talking about their art project, and how they'd wrapped the toys at school yesterday. Once he glanced at Joel, to see whether he minded that Elam was giving the news Joel had planned to tell. But Joel didn't care. All he really cared about was that Mom was going to be all right.

22. A Grateful Receiver

Mom had to be in hospital four days in all. The boys went to visit her twice more, once on Sunday and once on Monday after school. On Tuesday afternoon, Joel could hardly wait to get home. He ran ahead of Elam and dashed into the kitchen, banging the door.

Then he stopped short. A girl stood in front of him, holding a finger to her lips. It took Joel a moment to recognize Rachel Swartzentruber. "Sh-h-h," she said. "Your mom's asleep in the bedroom."

"Okay," said Joel. He went quietly upstairs to change. Then he fidgeted around in the kitchen, watching as Rachel peeled potatoes and swept the floor. "When do you think she's going to wake up?" he asked after awhile.

Rachel, who was merely sixteen, shrugged. "Better not wake her."

"'Course not." Joel watched her awhile longer. He wished Mom were working in the kitchen instead of Rachel. He wished . . . oh, he wished lots of things, but none of his wishes appeared to be coming true just now.

After Mom awoke, Joel went to her room. "Why is Rachel here?" was his first question.

"Because I'm not supposed to work yet," Mom answered with a smile. "We should be thankful she could come."

Joel wasn't so sure. He could remember when Rachel went to school, she had often been bossy with the younger children. Joel was in no mood to be bossed around, at least not by Rachel Swartzentruber. As a matter of fact, though, right now he wouldn't mind Mom bossing him a bit.

But Mom still wasn't much like her old self. Another week passed before she felt like "bossing" the boys again. One evening when they came home from school, Rachel was gone, and Mother was sitting at the sink with a paring-knife in her hand.

Joel beamed. "You're well again!"

Mom looked at him, barely smiling. "No, I'm afraid I'm not very well yet. I peeled one potato, and now I'm exhausted."

"Why did you let Rachel go then?" Joel blurted.

"Because her mom got sick, and she was needed at home." Mom put down the paring-knife. "I think I'll go to bed now. Maybe Elam can make potato soup for supper."

"Sure," said Elam confidently. He picked up the knife and a potato. Joel watched critically. His peelings were a lot thicker than Mom's, but at least he got the skin off. Then he began cutting the potato in chunks. "We should add some carrots to this soup. Get some in the cellar, Joel."

Joel did as he was told. Elam began peeling the carrot too.

"Mom doesn't peel carrots—she washes them!" Joel objected.

"Oh? How?"

Joel reached under the sink. "With this yellow brush."

Elam took the brush and scrubbed away. Then he

115

cut the carrot into orange coins and added them to the pot. "Now. Some water, I think. And salt." He put the pot on the woodstove. "Guess we could set the table while we wait for the soup to boil," he suggested.

When that was done, Elam checked the potatoes. "Hey! They haven't even started boiling!" he exclaimed.

Joel came over for a look. "What about the fire? Maybe it's low."

Elam opened the stove lid. A few red coals sat on the bottom of the grate. He peered into the wood box. "No wood! We better get busy." He dashed to the woodshed and split several pieces of wood. Soon they had the flames roaring up merrily. But it still seemed to take the potatoes a long time to boil. Elam kept poking them with a fork to see whether they were tender.

After awhile Mom came out of the bedroom. "Supper ready?" she asked with a little smile.

"Not quite. We forgot to get the fire going at first," Elam apologized.

"That's okay. I'll sit here till you have things ready." Mom eased herself onto a chair. "I do feel better now, after a little rest. I'm simply going to have to take it easy a while longer."

"Leave the work for us. We can do it," Elam assured her.

Mom patted his arm. "Yes, you can, and I'm thankful for my boys."

They had finished eating when someone knocked at the door. It was Sam Miller, Edwin's dad, and he was carrying a big, big box! He put the box on the table, took off his hat, and sat on a chair. "Well, how are things going?"

"Better, but slow," Mom told him.

"You still have help?"

"Yes—Joel and Elam," Mom replied with a smile.

Sam looked at the boys. "I guess you're old enough to be a good help too."

Joel was fidgeting. What could be in that huge box?

Sam grinned. "I guess you're wondering why I came. Well, the community got together a sunshine box for you folks. To help pass the winter months, you know, if you have to stay at home a lot." He patted the box. "There's a parcel in here for you to open every day from now through January."

"Something for every day?" Joel repeated, wide-eyed.

"That's right. It's nothing fancy, mind you. Just little things—mainly to remind you that people are thinking of you." Sam got to his feet. "Well, I better be going. Enjoy your sunshine box!"

"May we open a package now?" Joel asked eagerly when he was gone.

"Yes, if there's one with today's date."

Joel opened the big box and peered inside. "Yes, here's one for today." He lifted out a wide, flat package. "Now what could this be? It's from John Martins."

"Open it," suggested Mom.

Joel tore away the wrapping. "It's a calendar—a homemade calendar for next year!" he exclaimed. "My, these are nice pictures. Those Martin children are real artists. See, Elam?"

Elam didn't appear too interested. He took only one glance at the calendar, which was obviously the result of many hours of work.

"Well, it's not next year yet, but we could hang up the calendar anyway," said Mom. She was looking at Elam with a slight frown, but he refused to meet her eyes.

Joel loved that sunshine box! Every evening when the boys came home from school, they opened the day's package. Once there were some washcloths. Once there was a package of Jell-O. Another time it was macaroni. Once there was even a homemade game!

Joel kept offering to let Elam open a package, but Elam wasn't interested. He never exclaimed much over the contents of the packages either.

Finally Mom said to him, "Elam, don't you appreciate the neighbors' thoughtfulness?"

Elam scowled. "Well, what do they figure? That we can't take care of ourselves?"

"Oh, Elam, you must not let pride get in your way like that," Mom said with a shake of her head. "Think back to when you were making those presents for the orphans. You really enjoyed that, didn't you, doing something for someone else?"

Elam nodded grudgingly.

Mom went on, "The Bible says, 'God loveth a cheerful giver' (2 Cor. 9:7). And I've thought many times that those words might just as well be, 'God loveth a grateful receiver.'" She paused, then added in a low voice, "Elam, I know all too well that sometimes it's harder to be a receiver than a giver. But none of us could be givers if there were no receivers."

"You know, you're right," Elam agreed. "I hadn't

thought about it that way." He turned to Joel. "What did you say? May I open today's package?" Joel held it out to him. "You certainly may!"

23. Thirteenth Birthday

Little snow fell in January that year, but February quite made up for it. There was snow every day for the first two weeks. "I like having so much snow," Joel declared as Elam and he walked home from school one evening. He was shuffling along in the powdery drifts beside the road, making special tracks of his own.

"It's okay for now, but I hope it goes away in time for us to start planting in March," was Elam's reply.

"Thinking of the garden already?" Joel asked in surprise.

"Of course! Why, today's my birthday, and we usually make out our seed order weeks before that," Elam pointed out.

"You're right," Joel said thoughtfully. "I wonder why we haven't sent the order yet."

"Probably because of Mom's illness. But she's well now," Elam said.

Joel snapped his fingers as though remembering something. "Oh, yes! Remember what Mom said last year on your birthday?"

Elam wrinkled his brow. "No."

"She said you may start reading the Scripture for evening devotions when you're thirteen," Joel reminded him.

"That's right. I'd completely forgotten. Maybe Mom has forgotten too."

Joel shook his head. "I doubt it." He stamped his feet on the porch, then used the broom to sweep snow from his boots. The kitchen was warm and smelled invitingly of fresh-baked bread. Joel took one look at Mom's pink cheeks and exclaimed, "You look better than ever tonight."

Mom's color deepened even more. "Must be from the heat of the stove. I've been baking."

Joel stared longingly at the loaves of fresh brown bread. "Could we have a slice, with some butter and honey?"

"I guess so." Mom brought the bread knife and held the loaf carefully. "It's so easy to squash a fresh loaf. Here you are. Want some too, Elam?"

"Sure do."

Joel slathered his warm slice with butter and watched it melt down into the pores of the bread. Then he added some honey and sank his teeth into it. "M-m-m, this is good."

"Mom," said Elam, forgetting not to speak with his mouth full. "What about the seed order? Isn't it about time we fill it out?"

Mom was stooped down, taking something out of the oven. "Maybe we should," she said in a strange absent-minded way. "But not tonight. I have too many other things on my mind."

Whatever those things were, they must have still been on her mind when it was time for Scripture-reading that evening. Both boys waited expectantly when Mother brought the big German Bible. Joel was sure she would give it to Elam. After all, she hadn't forgotten it was his birthday.

But no, Mom opened the Bible herself. Joel couldn't keep quiet. "I thought you said Elam would do the reading once he's thirteen!"

Mom looked up. Once again her face was flushed. "Why, that's right. I forgot." She handed the Bible to Elam. "Here. We're ready for the last part of Luke 6. About the wise man and the foolish man."

Elam cleared his throat. Slowly he began to read. He stumbled a few times over the German words, but he could read almost as well as Mother. Joel tried to imagine that Elam was his dad, leading devotions as Harvey Yoder did.

Soon it was bedtime. Joel hunted around for his toothbrush. "Mom, where's my . . . " he began. Then, glancing at Elam, he raised his voice, "Why, you're using my toothbrush! Don't you know what color your own toothbrush is?" He swatted Elam's hand, intending to knock the toothbrush from his grip.

"Ow—ow!" roared Elam. "You needn't hit me! I didn't even know I had your brush."

"Boys," came Mom's voice, stern, but with a hint of weariness.

Joel felt instantly sorry. He knew Mom hated it when they quarreled.

Mom went on, "In the Scripture tonight, did you catch the difference between the wise man and the foolish man? Why was the wise man's house like one built on the rock, while the foolish man's was like one built on the sand?" Her eyes were on Joel.

"Why—uh, the wise man heard the Lord's words," he stammered.

"But the foolish man did too," Elam pointed out.

Joel felt his face grow hot. He realized he hadn't been paying proper attention.

Mom prompted, "You tell us then, Elam."

"The wise man also did as the Lord said. The foolish man merely heard the Lord's words but didn't do them," Elam explained.

Mother nodded. "Now remember all the things Jesus talked about earlier in Luke 6, such as doing unto others as you would have them do unto you. Jesus' words are no good to us unless we also put them into practice."

"Yes, Mother," Joel said. He went upstairs, still thinking about the house that crashed when the floods came.

In his room, he pressed his nose against the window, watching the snowflakes swirling out of the darkness. Thicker and faster they came, until the air seemed full of them. "No hurry for the seed order yet," Joel muttered to himself as he hurried to crawl under his warm blankets.

The sun was shining brightly next morning, its rays glinting on the fresh blanket of snow as the boys set off for school. Joel walked in a straight line, trying to keep his feet on tracks made by buggy wheels on the lane. Suddenly he stopped. "Elam! Was somebody here this morning? These tracks are fresh!"

Elam squinted against the sunlight. Between the two narrow tracks made by the wheels ran a horse's hoof prints. "How do you know they're fresh?"

"Because it was snowing when we went to bed. Really snowing!" Joel answered quickly.

"H-m-m-m. Nobody's been here that I know of, and I've been up since 6:30," Elam said thoughtfully.

Joel was getting excited. "Somebody must have been here during the night! Maybe it was a—a robber!

I'm going back to tell Mom."

Elam grabbed his arm. "Just a minute . . . just a minute! Tell me, what robber would come with a buggy? Are there Amish robbers?"

Joel stopped pulling to get away. "No, I guess not," he said sheepishly.

His practical big brother went on, "If you go back now, you'll be late for school. There'll be time enough to tell Mom about these tracks when we get home from school. Okay?"

"Okay," Joel agreed reluctantly. When they reached the end of the lane, he took careful note which way the buggy had turned. After all, you never knew. . . .

24. Great News

The door banged behind Joel as he dashed into the house after school. "Mom! Did you notice anything missing around here today?"

Mom turned to look at him with a quizzical frown. "Missing?"

"Well, there were buggy tracks in our lane this morning, and I figured anybody who would sneak in and out at night would be up to no good," Joel explained.

At that moment Elam came in and snorted, "So you still suspect an Amish thief?"

Joel glared at Elam, then turned back to Mom. She wore the strangest look—as though she didn't know whether to laugh or cry. Finally she sat down on the wood box and began to laugh.

Joel watched her in bewilderment. "What's the joke?"

Mom wiped her eyes. "I didn't know when would be the best time to tell you boys, but now is as good a time as any. Joel, Elam, . . . I have some important news."

Years afterward, Joel could still picture his mother the way she looked at that moment, sitting on the edge of the wood box, leaning forward earnestly. Her voice sounded strange—as though she wanted it to be firm, yet it refused to be firm.

Joel's heart started racing. Somehow he knew he

was about to hear something big and life-changing. Yet he was not prepared for what she said. "Boys, the man who was here last night came to visit me. He is . . . he is going to be your father."

Joel's thoughts churned. *How could that be? His own dad couldn't come back, and . . .*

"Mom!" exclaimed Elam. His voice squeaked, the way it often did these days because he was just starting to develop his grown-up voice. "You're getting married again!"

Joel's mind cleared a little. Of course. If Mother were to have a husband, he would have a father. "But—who?" he stammered.

Mother smiled. Her face had blushed a pretty pink color again. "George Detweiler."

Elam almost shouted, "Aaron and Allan's dad, you mean?"

"That's right."

Joel couldn't have been more surprised if Mom had hit him over the head. He groped for words. "Then if—George gets to be our dad, Aaron and Allan would be my brothers?"

"That's right," Mom said again. "So, along with your new dad, you are getting three brothers and two sisters."

Elam wrinkled his brow, trying to remember. "H-m-m. Oh, there's Peter and Pollyanna and . . . and . . ."

Mother supplied the other name for him. "Mary."

Elam smiled. "That will make two Marys in this house." Then his eyes opened wide as he thought of something. "Mom! Would we still live in this house? Or are we moving to Ohio to live at George's place?"

Joel thought his heart would stop. Move to Ohio?

Leave this house? Never. In the split second before Mom replied, Joel pictured Mom leaving for Ohio while he waved good-bye to her from the door of their house.

But Mother shook her head. "No, we won't be moving. George, Aaron, Allan and Mary want to come and live here. Peter and Pollyanna will stay on the farm in Ohio, and when Peter gets married, that will be his."

Joel hadn't realized he was holding his breath, but now he let out a long sigh.

Elam was full of questions. "Is that why you went to Ohio last fall, to visit George?"

"I guess that was the main reason," Mom admitted with a smile. "We saw each other several times that week."

Joel was remembering those buggy tracks in the snow. "But Mom, if that was George last night, did he come all the way from Ohio in a buggy?"

Elam fairly hooted. Mom's hand went to her mouth. She didn't want to embarrass Joel. "No. He stayed with relatives in the area over the weekend, and used someone else's buggy to come visit."

"I see," said Joel. Somehow he felt a little resentful toward Mom for doing something like this behind his back. "I hardly know how this George looks," he muttered.

"Oh," said Mom. "Well, his hair used to be the same color as the boys', if you remember what that was."

Joel nodded. "Reddish."

"Yes. Only it's all gray now."

"Is he pretty old?" Elam asked.

"Only 43," Mom replied. "Most men that age

aren't as gray as he is." She closed her eyes, probably picturing George. "What else could I say to describe him? He's tall—as tall as Harvey Yoder—but not as broad."

Elam was already thinking of something else. "Good thing we kept Will. Aaron will be glad!"

Mother nodded. "We're hoping that having Will here will help Aaron get used to his new home. He's the kind of boy who might find the changes difficult."

Joel was thinking, *What about me, Mom? How do you think I feel about getting a whole new family all of a sudden?* But of course he didn't say that out loud.

"Mom," Joel said. "You probably don't know George very well yet, if you've only seen him a few times." Joel was certain the wedding would still be a long way off. People had to know each other before they got married, didn't they?

But Mom asked, "Has it occurred to you that people can get to know each other quite well by writing letters? We've exchanged a lot of letters since . . . since last summer."

"Oh," said Joel. He was feeling miffed again. All those letters, and he never caught on! "Will this house have room for so many people?" he asked next.

"It may seem a little crowded at first," Mom admitted. "Aaron and Allan will need the one spare bedroom, and Mary the other. Perhaps sometime we'll add onto the house."

"When's the wedding?" asked practical Elam.

"In May. Actually, it's not so many weeks now till the Sunday when we're to be published. The whole

Detweiler family will be coming from Ohio that day. They will be staying at Harveys over the weekend. Then we can go back and forth and all get better acquainted. That will be nice, won't it?" Mom's voice had a pleading note to it.

Suddenly, Joel realized she wanted him and Elam to like them. All of them. The new dad, the new sisters. And the new brothers. Even Allan.

Something big and hard was pushing up into Joel's throat. He found himself wanting to run to Mother and bury his face in her apron and say, "Mom, let's just keep things the way they were. We liked it that way. We don't know whether we'll like the changes. Why not just stay the same as always?"

But he couldn't do that. He saw in Mom's face that this meant a great deal to her. He wanted her to be happy.

Joel looked down at himself and realized he was still wearing his school clothes. Just then the clock chimed five times. He got up and headed for the stairs. Mom must not see the tears that insisted on coming.

25. Brothers-to-Be

Later that evening, Mom got up from her rocking chair to go to bed. She paused on her way past the staircase. What was that sound?

She hurried softly up the stairs and knocked on the door to Joel's room. "Joel? May I come in?"

"Yes," said a muffled voice. The sobs she had heard were silent now.

Joel's bed creaked as she sat down on the edge. After a moment he felt her hand lightly touching his shoulder. She sat for awhile that way, not saying anything. He waited.

"Joel," she said, "do you think it's going to be hard?"

"I—I don't know."

"Maybe it is," she said. "Maybe I didn't think how hard it will be for you."

Joel held his breath. What would she say next, that she would just drop the whole matter, and they could go on as before? Then he felt ashamed of his selfish thought.

"Joel, tell me. Is it mostly because of the way you feel about Allan?"

Joel thought about it. "I guess I just don't like big changes."

"Changes are a part of life, Joel. Sooner or later, big changes do come. They come in different ways to different people. Not many people get new fathers,

130

of course. But everybody gets changes." Mom paused. "You are a little worried about having Allan for a brother, aren't you?"

Joel sniffed. "He made fun of our things."

"You know what I think? I think Allan didn't really mean to sound as scornful as you took him to be."

"Huh," said Joel.

The silence in the bedroom stretched on for so long that Joel began feeling guilty. He knew he was being difficult. He knew he should just be like Elam, matter-of-fact, taking everything in stride. But he was not Elam. He was Joel, an eleven-year-old boy facing something that looked impossible.

In the dim light Joel saw Mom reach a hand to her face. What was she doing? Wiping away a tear? Joel gulped. "Mom, I don't mean to make things hard for you. I'm glad if you're happy."

Mom's hand squeezed his shoulder. "I want you to be happy too, Joel. I would not be doing this—we would not be getting married—unless we believed it is what God wants. Do you believe that too?"

"Yes."

"I guess," Mother went on, her voice growing less shaky again, "it all comes back to being willing, doesn't it? We have to be willing to accept changes. Willing to make adjustments. Willingness makes it easier all along the way."

A slow smile spread across Joel's face. Talking about willingness made him think of Will—the horse that needed a carrot to get him going. There was a chuckle in Joel's voice now as he said, "Mom, we don't want to be like Will, do we?"

Mom patted his shoulder. "That's my boy. No, we

certainly don't. Ready to sleep now?"

"Yes, Mother." His eyes closed, and he fell asleep almost before Mom reached the bottom step. In his dreams, Allan Detweiler rode Will at full gallop down the pasture. Then Will stepped into a ground-hog hole, and Allan flew over the horse's head and fell into the creek. When Allan came out of the creek, he was shaking his red hair, just the way Jim did when he was through with a swim.

Weeks passed. Warm weather came, and with it the seed order Mom and the boys had sent off. Soon Joel was so busy helping plant garden that he didn't have much time to think about the Detweilers.

Finally, though, the day came for Mother and George to be published. A feeling of dread grew inside Joel as he and Mom and Elam neared the place where church was being held that Sunday morning. What should he say to his red-haired brothers-to-be when he saw them? How would Allan act? Aaron was sure to smile—but what about Allan? Joel's dread grew until it threatened to choke him.

Lady slowed to a walk as they drove in the lane behind a half-dozen other buggies. "I guess we should have taken Will this morning," Elam remarked. "Aaron is sure to ask about him."

"Aaron can see Will when they all come to our place this afternoon," Mom replied before leaving the buggy.

Shortly after Elam had tied Lady, Aaron Detweiler appeared around the corner of the barn. A wide grin spread across his face. "Hello," he said shyly.

Elam and Joel smiled and nodded.

Then Allan came. "Hello," he said abruptly. He jammed his hands into his pockets. "Nice sunny day."

"Yes," agreed Elam. "Shall we go in?"

Joel took a deep breath. It was over—that first dreaded encounter. Somehow, though, they would have to spend the whole afternoon and evening together. And later, after the wedding, they would spend a lifetime together, he and these boys who were almost strangers. Then Joel pushed the thought away. For now, at least, everything was all right.

After the church service and lunch were over, Mom and the boys went home. Soon the Detweilers joined them, and Joel and Elam met the Detweiler girls. Mary had light brown hair and freckles on her nose. Her eyes were green like her dad's. There was something about her smile that made Joel think of mischief.

Pollyanna seemed to be like Aaron—shy and quiet. Her hair was not red though, but black. Peter was a lot like his twin, only in a boyish sort of way.

"Shall we go outside?" Elam asked the younger boys.

Allan shrugged. Aaron asked with shy eagerness, "Can we see Will?"

"Sure." Elam led the way to the barn. Allan seemed reluctant but came too.

"Do you still use him sometimes?" Allan asked once they stood in front of Will's stall. His voice implied that *he* certainly wouldn't be using him!

Elam replied, "He has cultivated the garden a few times this spring."

"Pretty slow, I guess?" Allan looked at Joel.

Joel nodded. He didn't trust himself to say anything. He kept his eyes on Aaron, who was talking to Will. The horse was unmistakably delighted to see Aaron!

After awhile Allan said impatiently, "Have you seen enough of that horse now?"

Aaron shook his head.

Allan turned to Elam, "Come on. Let's you and I go out, if he wants to stay with Unwilling all day."

Elam hesitated. He knew it wouldn't be polite to leave Aaron alone in the barn. "You staying here?" he asked Joel.

Joel nodded and watched them go with a sense of relief. He knew things weren't exactly the way you would expect, with the older Stutzman going off with the younger Detweiler while he, Joel, stayed with fourteen-year-old Aaron. But it was a very comfortable arrangement as far as Joel was concerned!

After supper was over, and the Detweilers had gone, Joel asked Elam, "What did you and Allan do?"

"Oh, we went for a walk. Allan wanted to see the cave."

"He did?" Joel exclaimed in surprise. "And he didn't make fun of it?"

"He said something about it being pretty small, but I didn't mind," Elam said with a shrug.

Joel scowled. "So he did make fun of it."

Mom looked up from her book. "Elam didn't feel that way about it, Joel. Have you ever heard that saying, 'Beauty is in the eye of the beholder'? Perhaps it would also be right to say, 'Scorn is in the ear of the hearer.' It helps to not expect Allan to be scornful."

"I see," said Joel, though he wasn't sure that he did. One thing, at least, was sure: he liked Aaron. The girls and Peter were probably all right too. As for Allan, well, only time would tell.

26. Changes

Joel lay on his stomach on the cool earth floor of the cave. His one arm was stretched out so his hand hung in the creek. The water tickled his fingers as it eddied past the roots of the cedar tree.

Jim had been sniffing around in the back of the cave, but now he came and flopped down beside Joel. His tongue hung out as he smiled a collie smile. Joel scratched Jim's ruff with his other hand.

Joel sighed. It was a half-happy, half-sad sigh. It felt good to be here in the cool, quiet cave with the creek rippling past. That made him happy. But when his thoughts traveled up through the pasture to the house, he was sad.

Or was it sadness he felt? Joel wasn't sure. All he knew was that it wasn't a good feeling to think of all the new people that had crowded into his life since the wedding. The once roomy house was suddenly too small. There was no privacy anywhere, not even in the garden or the barn. Wherever Joel went, there was George—or Allan—or Aaron—or Mary. Life was just not the same anymore.

Lying there in the cool cave, Joel thought back to the wedding. How strange it had seemed, to see his mother getting married! In a way it hadn't seemed real. Not on the wedding day, anyway.

But now it was reality. Moving day had come and gone. The house seemed to have twice as much furniture in it as before. Everywhere he looked, Joel saw changes. The livestock in the barn was no longer Harvey's. It was George's. The crops in the fields, Mom had said, were not Harvey's either. She had paid for the seed grain, and now the crops belonged to them, to Mom and George. *To us,* Elam had said firmly.

Joel buried his face in Jim's soft fur. "I don't feel like it's 'us,'" he told the dog. "They don't seem like my family. George isn't my dad."

A tear escaped and was quickly lost in Jim's golden coat. "How does Elam do it?" Joel went on. "He acts as though getting a new family is the most everyday thing in the world!"

Very faintly, Joel heard a voice, Mom's voice, calling, "Jo-o-el!" He sat up with a start. He knew he should be up there, helping pick berries. He started to climb out.

Then he stopped and lay down in the cave again. Beside him, Jim thumped his tail as if to say, *I understand. I know how you feel. You can count on me.*

As Joel touched the dog, he thought of Aaron. He remembered the way Aaron looked when he was with Will. "I guess he needs Will the way I need Jim," Joel said out loud.

Jim's tail thumped harder. He licked Joel's hand.

Then Mom's voice drifted to them again. "Jo-o-o-el!"

"Guess I better go," Joel grunted as he scrambled up. "She might start getting anxious." He hurried up through the pasture.

Mom was standing on the porch, shading her eyes against the sun. "Where were you?" she asked sharply.

137

Joel's heart ached. Her voice had been like that more than once the last while—sharp, with an edge to it. To Joel it seemed that Mom was not the mom she used to be. Everything was changing and nothing, it seemed, was changing for the better!

"Oh, just somewhere. What do you want?" he mumbled.

Mom's tone turned gentle. "There are lots of berries to pick, Joel. And we need lots of help, enough help so we can free Elam to do some cultivating. The weeds are growing so fast over by the tomatoes." She spoke quickly and brightly, as though hoping to chase away Joel's gloom.

But Joel refused to let his gloom be chased. He hung onto it as he started picking berries. He refused to be cheered by the fact that Mary was a good picker. So was Allan, for that matter.

Then Joel saw Elam and Aaron hitching Will to the cultivator. Suddenly he was jealous. So jealous that he said to Mom, who was picking nearby, "That used to be my job."

"Which job?" Mother was puzzled.

"Leading the horse for cultivating," Joel replied, his voice showing how hurt he felt.

"Why, Joel!" Mom was so surprised that she sat back on her heels and looked at him. "I thought you never liked that job, so I suggested Aaron could do it."

Joel felt his face grow hot. Mom was right, of course. Had he ever cultivated the garden without complaining? Probably not. Yet now, when his new brother was about to do it for him, he was jealous. Joel was too ashamed to say a word.

Then Mom said pleasantly, "Aaron will be happy

to pick berries, if you'd rather lead Will."

Joel shook his head. The hurt and confusion inside him was threatening to spill over in tears. On top of everything else, this made him angry at himself. Why did he have to be such a big baby, anyway? All the others seemed to be adjusting without a hitch.

Soon he heard Mom chuckling. He looked up sharply. Was she laughing at him? That would be the last straw. Mom never used to laugh at him. At least, never if she knew it would hurt him.

But Mom was pointing across the garden. "Just look at Will! It looks as though we have a new horse."

Joel turned his head to look. Then he sat back in amazement. Was that Will? Aaron was leading him, and Will's head was up. He was lifting his feet high, and he was pulling the cultivator so fast that Elam could hardly keep up!

"All because of Aaron, I suppose," Mother said softly. "I think Aaron must know a secret button to push on that horse somewhere."

Joel nodded. He watched the cultivating for a moment longer, then turned back to his berry-picking. Seeing Aaron with Will had chased part of his gloom away.

But the gloom came back that evening. Evenings had changed too. For one thing, there were more barn chores to do, and so it was usually later by the time everybody was through. For another thing, George led devotions now. Actually, Joel liked that. It seemed right and proper to have a deep, strong man's voice reading the Scriptures.

It was what came after devotions that Joel

missed. Or, more correctly, what didn't come afterwards any more. Before, that had been a special time when Joel, Elam, and Mom often sat and talked together. They would talk about ordinary things like garden, school, or wood supply, or they would share concerns. It was during these times that Joel learned what God meant to Mom. She spoke of Him as her best Friend and her Helper for whatever she needed.

Now, of course, with a bunch of strangers thrown together in their living room, such special times were a thing of the past. Devotions tended to be quite formal, and right afterwards it was bedtime.

As he lay in bed that evening, Joel said to himself, "I think I know what the hardest part is for me. It's never having Mom to myself anymore. She belongs to George now, and besides, she has three times as many children to look after as before! No wonder she has no time left for me."

He could feel sobs pushing at his throat, but he didn't dare let them come. Nothing but a thin wall separated him from Aaron and Allan in the next room.

27. Aaron's Hayloader

For the first while after the "Big Change," as Joel thought of it, mealtimes tended to be quiet and even a little strained. Mom and George spoke to each other every now and then. But there was no happy chatter from the boys, or from Mary, for that matter. She and Aaron sat looking like timid rabbits. Allan wasn't timid. Sometimes he made faces at Mary, who sat across from him.

One day at dinnertime, Mom and George were discussing something. Suddenly Mary screeched.

Seven pairs of eyes stared at Mary. Most of the eyes looked shocked—except for Allan's. His eyes were dancing with mischief.

Joel glanced at George. His usually friendly, green eyes were quite stern now. So was his voice. "Mary! Allan! What was that all about?"

"Allan kicked me," Mary said faintly.

George focused on Allan. "You must learn to act decently at the table."

Allan nodded and mumbled, "Sorry."

George's mouth shut in a straight line, and he said no more. If the atmosphere had been strained before, it was doubly so now. Joel stared unhappily at the piece of pie on his plate. He wasn't sure he could eat it all.

After awhile, Mother tried to break the tension. "It's nice being done with berries by noon, isn't it,

141

boys? Last year we used to be at it practically all day."

"Yes," said Elam, when nobody else volunteered to say anything.

Mother went on in the same bright voice, "What are you boys going to do this afternoon? I guess there is no hay ready."

Joel looked at Elam. Elam looked at Allan. Allan looked at his plate.

It was Aaron who saved the uncomfortable situation. "Dad, have you unpacked your shop tools?"

"I unpacked the last ones yesterday. They're all in that little room off the shed with the workbench," his dad replied.

"We could make something," Aaron said hopefully, looking at Elam and Joel.

"Sure," said Elam. After dinner he and Aaron headed for the shop. Joel followed more slowly. Allan disappeared.

"What can you make?" Elam asked Aaron.

"I once made a toy hayloader, but it broke," Aaron offered.

Elam was enthusiastic. "Let's make one again! Did it really work?"

Aaron nodded. "A little. We loaded grass clippings onto a toy wagon with it. We cranked it by hand."

Joel followed them into the shop. He looked around with a feeling of pleasure. What a lot of tools there were, everything a boy could need to make something! Mom never had many tools. She used to say Dad didn't need many. He wasn't a handyman. Other people had to repair things and make things for him.

My new dad, Joel thought, *must be different. And*

Aaron is too. Joel watched in fascination as Aaron took some scrap lumber and set to work.

"Spools," said Aaron. "I'm going to need spools, the kind for thread."

"There are lots in the toy box. I'll get some." Joel hurried to the house. When he came out again with his hands full of spools, Allan was standing on the porch.

"What have you got there?" Allan's voice was hard.

"Spools," replied Joel. Suddenly his knees were weak.

"What for?" demanded Allan.

Joel's voice trembled. "Aaron is making a hayloader."

"A hayloader!" hooted Allan. "Last time he made one, it fell apart."

Joel lifted his chin. He was scared, but a little angry too. "What does that matter?" he asked defensively.

"'What does that matter?'" mimicked Allan, making his voice sound just as scared and angry as Joel's. "'What does that matter?'"

Joel turned and walked towards the shop. Tears of rage burned his eyelids. Why, oh, why, had Mother brought this horrid boy into his life?

As he went into the shop, Joel thought, *Yet I'm glad Aaron is here. And I couldn't have Aaron without Allan.*

Aaron took the spools and began fastening them to his little rack with a piece of wire. Joel could see that Elam was just as fascinated as he. It was really something to watch Aaron's hands at work. His nimble fingers seemed to know just what to do.

Before long Aaron said, "There. Now, do you have a toy wagon? A shoe box will do, too."

"How about a nail box?" Elam asked, holding one up.

Aaron nodded. He picked up his little creation. Joel had to admit it looked as though it could fall apart. Aaron cradled it carefully as they went out to the lawn.

"Now we have to pull some grass and arrange it in windrows, like this." Aaron put down the hay-loader and began pulling grass. Soon Elam and Joel were helping too.

"Now," said Aaron. "Where is that nail box?" Carefully he hung the loader onto the box. With his fingers he coaxed the spools to go around. Jerkily the wires climbed up the rack. Aaron had to help the wisps of grass hang onto the wires. All in all, it was a fairly shaky business, but it worked! Some grass did make its way into that nail box as Aaron inched it along the makeshift windrows.

"That's great," Joel said enthusiastically. "I couldn't have thought up something like that."

Aaron looked up from his hay making. His face glowed.

Then suddenly their little bubble of happiness burst. Allan came around the corner of the shop. He took one look at Aaron's creation and asked, "What kind of toy is that?"

Aaron looked at his brother fearfully. "Don't! Please don't," Aaron pleaded.

But Allan drew back his foot and kicked the little hayloader. It flew across the grass, and landed in ruins.

"Allan! What have you done?"

144

All four boys whirled. There stood Allan's dad. Joel cringed. Allan cowered. Dad's iron voice said, "Come with me." Allan followed very meekly.

After they were gone, the other three boys sat on the grass, not daring to look at one another. Joel whispered, "What do you think will happen to Allan?"

"He's getting a thrashing." Aaron seemed absolutely sure.

A jolt went through Joel. Twelve years old, and getting a spanking? Why, the last time Mom had spanked Joel must have been two or three years ago.

Cold fear clutched at Joel's stomach. If George was spanking Allan, that meant he might spank Joel too!

Aaron seemed to guess what Joel was thinking. He reached over to pat Joel's arm. "Don't be scared. He won't spank you unless you're bad."

"I—I'm not scared," Joel denied. But he was, so scared his teeth were almost chattering.

145

28. Hay Making

"There's a lot of hay ready for today," George announced the next morning at the breakfast table. "I expect I will be raking most of the morning, while the rest of you pick berries."

Seventeen-year-old Mary spoke up eagerly. "May I help rake too? I could use the other team, and—and we could borrow Harvey's rake."

Joel looked at her in surprise. He had never seen her so eager. A girl, all excited about raking hay?

Mary's dad did not appear surprised, but he shook his head. "Harveys will be using their rake too. That's the trouble—we both have hay for today. We tried to stagger things so that only one or the other of us has hay. But the rain threw our schedule off." He paused, running his eyes over the children. "You must all work fast with the berries this morning. We will need lots of helpers with the hay this afternoon."

Joel tingled with excitement. How often he had wished for a chance to help with the haying! Now the time had come. He did wonder, though, what there would be left for him to do, if even the girls helped.

Aaron's dad had it all planned out by noon. "I talked with Harvey," he said as they ate dinner, "and we decided we would each work on our own hay this time. They have a hayloader and two wagons; so do

146

we. They have lots of help; so do we!" He smiled at everybody. "Aaron, you can help with the loading. Allan, you are good in the haymow. Elam, do you have any experience running the hayfork up in the barn?"

"Not much," Elam admitted, then added hastily, "but I can learn."

"I'm sure you can." Then his green eyes rested on Joel. "How do you feel about driving the team in the field?"

Joel trembled. "I haven't driven a team very much."

"Mary, I think you would make a good teacher for a young lad like Joel," her dad said.

Mary's face glowed. "I would enjoy showing him."

We'll be like one big machine. We each have to do our part to make it work, Joel thought happily as he finished his pie.

As Allan passed Joel on the porch a few minutes later, he nudged him with his elbow and whispered derisively, "You need a girl to teach you how to drive a team!" Joel's happiness was gone, burst like a soap bubble in the air.

Yet he couldn't help being fascinated by Mary's way with horses. She was completely unafraid. Joel was awed by these horses, like mountains of muscle and energy. The Detweilers had brought two matching, light-brown teams, all with golden manes and tails.

Mary and Allan hitched up Jerry and Bill while Joel watched. Then Mary climbed onto the wagon, calling out, "Let's go, Joel!"

Joel hesitated. He glanced at Allan who grinned mockingly. But Allan's dad was not far away, fastening the hayloader to the wagon. Joel swallowed his embarrassment and climbed on. He clung to the front ladder of the rack as Mary clucked to the horses. They were off!

"For the first few loads, you can ride along and watch," Mary told him kindly. "That will give you an idea how to follow the windrows and all that."

Joel nodded. He could see Mary loved what she was doing. Her eyes shone as she handled the reins, guiding those big horses with only a slight pull to the right or left.

"Jerry and Bill are very gentle," Mary assured Joel. "Their mouths are not hard, so they're easy to guide. Besides, they know all about haymaking!"

Joel managed a crooked smile. "They probably know more than I do."

"You'll learn," Mary said encouragingly.

And he did. Mary's dad was right—she was a good teacher. Before long, Joel felt quite comfortable with the reins. He also began to feel comfortable with Mary. It wasn't hard to chat with her as they perched on the loads of hay and drove back and forth. "You know," she confided, "I was afraid I wouldn't get to help work in the fields anymore with two more brothers in the family."

Joel looked at her. *It wasn't easy for her to become part of a new family, either.* The thought was like a bond between them. "I'm glad you can teach me to handle the workhorses," he said shyly.

She smiled at him, and the bond was complete. Suddenly Joel realized he was glad he had a sister!

By suppertime all the hay had been gathered in. "Everybody worked well," Father praised the family as they ate. Joel felt good all over.

The good feeling lingered later on, after Joel had

done his chores in the barn. Spying Mom alone in the garden, he went over to her. "Doing some weeding?" he asked.

"Yes. I could use your help," she replied.

They worked in silence for a few minutes. Joel thought, *Here I am, alone with Mom at last, and I can't think of anything to say.* Then he remembered Aaron's hayloader. "Mom, Aaron made a little hayloader yesterday."

"I heard about that."

"Who told you?"

Mom smiled at Joel. "Moms and dads tell each other everything, you know."

Joel thought about that. He still hadn't gotten used to Mom calling George "Dad." He said, "I guess moms and dads like each other a lot." Inside, he felt a twinge of jealousy.

"Joel," asked Mom, "do you like yourself?"

"Of course." He was mystified.

"Well, you see, the Bible says that when a man and a woman get married, it's sort of like they become one person. They are part of each other. So for a mom to like a dad is simply to like herself."

"Oh." Somehow, this did not help Joel's jealousy.

Mom went on, "But I want you to know that a mom and dad's love for each other doesn't take away any of their love for their children. Not one little bit. In fact, the more they love each other, the more they can love their children."

"Oh," said Joel again, feeling a little better. "You found out that Allan got a thrashing too?"

Mom looked at him. "Did that make you afraid?"

"Yes," he admitted. "You never spanked us anymore."

Mother's voice was firm. "A spanking comes from a father's love for his son. Remember the verse from Hebrews 12, 'For whom the Lord loveth he chasteneth'? You and your brothers may be thankful you have a father who loves you enough to chasten you."

"Yes, Mother," said Joel. He felt a new respect for George as he thought over what Mom had said. After pulling pigweeds in silence for a while, he asked, "Mom, why is Allan so often bad, even if he knows his dad will spank him?"

Mother sighed. "I don't know, Joel. It may be because he is having a hard time adjusting to these big changes in his life. I guess it shows up for different people in different ways. We all have to make adjustments, don't we? And maybe it's a little harder for Allan than for the rest of us."

Somehow, Joel found that hard to believe. To him, Allan seemed like a tough character, not somebody who would have a hard time adjusting.

"You and Allan don't always get along, I guess," Mom said with another little sigh.

Joel shook his head. "He keeps watching for any chance to make fun of me."

"Try not to let it bother you so much," Mother advised. "And remember what Jesus said. 'Pray for them that despitefully use you.'"

"Yes," Joel said guiltily. He knew he hadn't been doing as Jesus said. So when he knelt by his bed that evening, Joel prayed, "Help Allan and me to get along better. And help us be good."

29. Another Lesson in Willingness

Right from the beginning, it seemed to Joel the day was off to a bad start. On his way downstairs for breakfast, Allan sped past him and hissed something. Joel didn't even understand what he said, but he was convinced it wasn't anything nice.

All morning, out in the garden, Joel tried to avoid Allan. Whenever they were near each other, he looked the other way. How mixed-up Joel felt! Only last night he had prayed for Allan. He knew he should not be feeling this way toward his new brother. But he did. He wished he had never, never seen Allan Detweiler.

There were so many berries that berry-picking was not finished by noon. At the table, George said, "Mom, I guess the boys and I shouldn't all go to Harveys this afternoon, with so many berries left to pick. Would you like two of the boys to stay here?"

"That might be a good idea," replied Mother with a nod.

George's eyes traveled around the table. He smiled at all the boys. Then he said, "Joel and Aaron, you may stay home to help Mom and Mary with the berries."

Joel was stunned. He almost opened his mouth to object. In the old days, if Mom had said something that seemed unfair, he would have argued. But he didn't dare argue with his stepfather.

151

Joel glanced at Allan. There was a look of glee on his face—and no wonder! Allan got to help with the hay, while Joel had to stay home, bent double in the garden.

Joel was seething inside. After dinner he made sure to stay far away from Allan, who was bound to rub in his good fortune if he had the chance. Soon George, Elam, and Allan brought out the team and rumbled off to Harveys with the hay wagon.

Aaron was his usual sunny self when he came out to the garden. "I like berry-picking," he remarked cheerfully as he stooped down on the other side of Joel's row.

Joel didn't say a word for fear his anger would spill out. He didn't want Aaron to know how angry he was. Maybe it was because Aaron himself never seemed to get angry.

After awhile Joel grumbled, "I wonder why Mom and Mary don't come out to help?"

"Mary's washing dishes," Aaron explained. "And I think Mom is taking a nap."

"A nap!" Joel exploded. "Mom didn't used to take naps—not in the busy berry season, anyway."

Minutes ticked by. The sun seemed to grow hotter and hotter. Still Mary and Mother did not come. Joel found himself growing resentful. "Listen," he said, sitting back on his heels. "I don't see why we should be working so hard in the hot sun when no one else is."

Aaron looked up quizzically.

An idea had taken root in Joel's mind. "Let's go somewhere where it's cool, to the cave!"

Aaron frowned. "But Dad said we're to pick berries."

Joel hesitated. Would Aaron's dad punish him?

Would he dare? After all, George wasn't his dad—or was he?

Joel bent down and picked a few more berries. Then he straightened up again. "I'm going," he said decisively. "Even if you're not. It's not fair that we have to pick berries." He started off across the garden, heading for the pasture.

Slowly, Aaron stood up. He looked toward the house. Then he looked at Joel. After a moment he followed slowly.

It took them only a few minutes to reach the cave. How welcome was its cool shade! The two boys sat side by side on the old couch. Neither of them felt much like talking.

Joel was busy thinking though. He was trying to sort out his mixed-up feelings. He was remembering how, months ago, he used to wish he were part of a big family, like Harveys. And he used to wish he had a father.

Now his wish had come true. He had a father, and two sisters, and three brothers. But instead of being glad, he was unhappier than ever! It just didn't make sense.

Along with his unhappiness, Joel was starting to feel guilty. The longer he sat there on the couch, the guiltier he felt. He had disobeyed his stepfather. And in so doing, he had probably disobeyed Mom as well.

Aaron was the first to say something. "Shall we go back to the garden now?"

Joel nodded wordlessly and got to his feet. As they went up through the pasture, they could hear Mother calling, "Jo-el! Aa-ron!"

"Here we come," Aaron called back cheerfully.

Joel felt anything but cheerful. Would Mother

153

scold him? How could he bear that—a scolding on top of all his unhappiness?

But Mother didn't scold. She just looked at him in a sad questioning way that made Joel feel worse. He was miserable the rest of the afternoon. It would have been easier if she had scolded him.

Finally it was supper time and the men came home. Joel never found out when Mother told George about the afternoon. But after supper George said gravely, "Aaron and Joel, I want you to come with me."

Fear choked Joel's throat. He followed his stepfather to the woodshed. George sat down on a big chunk of firewood. "I hear you were disobedient." His voice was as grave as his face.

Aaron nodded. Joel stood there without moving.

"You will have to be punished. Mother and I love you and want you to learn to obey. Come, Aaron."

Joel wanted to call out, *Don't punish him! It was my fault. I made him go.* But he could not find his voice. Tears streamed down his face as Aaron received his whipping.

Then it was Joel's turn. After it was over, George put an arm around each of them and drew them close.

The feeling inside Joel was new to him. What was it? He had thought he would be angry if Allan's dad spanked him, but he wasn't. Nor was he afraid anymore. Instead, there was relief—and respect—and willingness. Willingness to obey this man. Never before had he felt so close to his stepfather.

30. Mom and Dad

Rain fell that night. Berry-picking the next morning was a muddy business. "My trousers are all muddy," Joel remarked across the row to Elam.

"So are mine," Elam replied cheerfully. "Well, the berries needed another rain."

Joel nodded. "This way we won't need to water them, at least."

Elam glanced at Aaron and Allan who were picking several rows away. "Allan is a good picker. If he didn't reach across the middle and do more than half the row, I think he'd be way ahead of Aaron."

Joel said nothing. He didn't feel like talking about Allan's good points. At the same time, he realized it wasn't right to feel that way. Remembering his conversation with Mother a few days ago, he said, "Mom thinks part of the reason Allan is bad so often is because it's been hard for him to make all these changes."

Elam looked at him. "You don't believe that?"

Joel shrugged. "I don't know."

"Well, I believe it. Because the changes are hard for me too."

"For you?" Joel exclaimed. He'd thought Elam was sailing along, cheerfully taking all the new things in stride.

"Yes," responded Elam. "Did you think you are the only one scared of Allan? And sometimes I'm a little scared of Dad too."

Joel didn't know what to say. In a way it made him feel good to know this. In another way, he wanted to help Elam too. He told him what Mom had said about moms and dads loving their children. "There's a verse in the Bible that says fathers spank their children because they love them, you know."

"Yes, I know," Elam responded with a nod. Then he looked up. "Somebody's walking in the lane. Joe Yoder, I think."

"Wonder what he wants?" Joel said curiously. "He's talking with Mom now."

Joe left again soon. Shortly afterwards, Joel purposely walked past Mom with a load of berries. "What did Joe want?"

"He came to tell us Ella Miller died. You know, Edwin's grandmother who had cancer." Mom got to her feet. "I'm going to find Dad. We'll probably go to the Millers this afternoon."

"Why?" asked Joel.

"To help prepare for the funeral." Mom looked at him. "I guess we haven't had a funeral in our neighborhood for quite a few years. Maybe none you would remember. Neighbors always go help when somebody dies."

"Oh," said Joel. "So when my dad died, the neighbors came here?"

"Yes, they came and were very kind." She patted his shoulder. "That was a long time ago." Then she walked toward the barn in search of the man she called "Dad" now. Joel knew they wanted him to call George "Dad" too. Somehow, though, he hadn't felt like it yet.

At the dinner table Mom said, "Mary, we'll probably

156

be away when Mr. Johnson comes. I expect he'll take most of the berries that are left. He gets them for ten cents a quart less because he takes so many."

"All right," Mary said with a nod. "What should we do with the leftover berries if he doesn't take them all?"

"Hull them for canning, I guess. We should be home before supper, so I can help with the canning."

Before he left, George instructed the boys to clean out some pigpens. He also warned, "I want you to work together peacefully."

And they did. As usual, Allan worked vigorously and got more done than the others. Joel was afraid Allan would call him a slow worker, but he didn't.

They were almost finished when Elam said, "What was that? It sounded like thunder."

All four manure forks paused as the boys cocked their heads to listen. Sure enough, there was a flash of lightning, then a loud rumble of thunder. "Another shower," commented Allan as he set to work again.

Joel had a funny feeling in his stomach. He wasn't exactly afraid of thunderstorms. At the same time, he preferred having grownups around during one. Yet here they were, five children alone on the farm, and a storm coming rapidly closer.

"Guess we're done now. Shall we go in?" Elam suggested.

Joel wanted to say eagerly, "Yes, let's!" But he didn't, because he was afraid Allan might think him a baby.

Allan hung up his fork. "We might as well," he said carelessly. Rain had begun to fall, and the boys pelted through the barnyard as fast as they could.

Thunder rumbled directly overhead as they reached the house. Joel's breath came in gasps. He stood close to the kitchen stove, shivering.

"I'll stir up the fire to dry out your clothes," Mary offered. She opened the stove and put in some kindling. "There, you'll soon be warmer now," she smiled at Joel.

Joel smiled back nervously. He knew his shivers were not all from being cold.

Perhaps Mary knew that too. At any rate, she suggested, "Shall I read aloud? I found such an interesting book, and I think you would all enjoy it."

"Please do!" begged Aaron. He wasn't good at reading himself, but he loved when someone read to him. He sat down near Mary on the couch.

Mary held up her book, *More Stories from Grandma's Attic.* "Maybe you boys have read all the stories in here." She looked at Elam and Joel.

"Yes, we have, but that doesn't matter," Joel said quickly. He, too, was eager for Mary to read aloud. That way he wouldn't mind the thunder so much.

"My, it's dark. Shall I light a lamp?" Mary asked.

"A lamp? At three o'clock in the afternoon?" Allan exploded.

Joel held his breath, hoping Mary would go ahead. A light would help shut out the lightning flashes too.

"Well, you have to agree it's dark enough," Mary said as she lifted the lamp's chimney and held a match to the wick.

Joel pulled his chair closer to the couch. There in the pool of lamplight he felt secure from the rising wind and booming thunder. Mary's voice was soothing as she read aloud. *It's nice having a big sister,* Joel thought.

Gradually the storm faded into the distance, and the sky began to brighten. Mary stopped reading. "I don't think we need the light any longer," she said. With a quick puff, she blew it out.

Aaron went to the window. "Dad and . . . and Mom will probably come home now that the rain has stopped."

Joel joined him, staring out to the road. There was no one coming. He began to watch the clouds. The thunderheads were dwindling away into the southeast. Then he looked toward the northwest. "Look at that!" he exclaimed. "Must be another storm coming."

Huge clouds, even darker than the first ones, were boiling up from the horizon and blotting out the patch of blue that had been showing.

"Dad and Mom had better hurry," Aaron observed.

The storm approached swiftly. The first clap of thunder was so loud it made Joel jump. He glanced over his shoulder to see whether Allan had noticed. Fortunately, Allan's nose was buried in a book.

Elam came to the window too. "I wonder whether Mom and Dad have started off for home?"

"They'll get caught in the storm," Joel said apprehensively.

"If they do, they'll stop in somewhere till it's over. Don't you worry," Elam assured him.

But Joel did worry. *What if something should happen to Mom? What if . . . ?* He tried not to think about the things that could happen.

Once more Mary lit the lamp as the kitchen grew shadowy. Aaron begged for another story, and Mary read again. This time, though, Joel didn't listen as well. He was too busy thinking about Mom out there in the storm somewhere.

After what seemed a long time, the thunder quieted down. Joel hurried to the window. A buggy was driving up the road. It was . . . yes, it was Lady! Joel's voice was almost a shout. "Here they come! Here come Mom and Dad!"

He felt his face grow warm. Without thinking, he'd called them "Mom and Dad." He wondered whether the others had noticed.

But nobody had, because they were all so glad to see Mom and Dad coming home.

31. Closer Than a Brother

There were showers every day for the next six days. The rain was good for the strawberries; even the late-season berries stayed large and juicy. But rain was not good for the hay. It lay in damp rows in the field, turning blacker and soggier every day.

"I wish the sun would shine," Joel complained to Elam one afternoon. They were standing in the hay-field, staring at the sad-looking windrows.

"The sun shone yesterday," Elam pointed out.

"Yes. Then it rained again last night," replied Joel. "I wish we could make hay. That way we'd know what to do. It's hard to know what to play with Aaron and Allan."

Elam nodded, but didn't say anything. After awhile he turned back to the barn. Joel followed. Aaron came running across the lawn to the barn.

"He seems excited about something," Joel commented.

"Let's find out what he's after," Elam said as he yanked open the barn door.

Aaron was heading for Will's stall. "I'm going to ride Will!" he said excitedly. "Dad said I may."

"Will you ride him on the road?" Elam wondered.

"Oh, no. Just in the pasture. Have you ever ridden bareback?" Aaron asked. He was in the stall now, putting a halter on Will.

"I used to ride one of Harvey's work horses."

161

Elam replied. "But we never rode Lady. Mother didn't want us to."

Joel had never ridden a horse, but he didn't say so. He watched as Aaron led Will from his stall.

"I used to ride Will when we had him. This used to be his riding halter," Aaron said enthusiastically.

The barn door opened, and Allan came inside. He stared at Aaron and Will. "So! You're going to take a ride on Will the unwilling?"

"He's not unwilling," Aaron said mildly. "Come on, Will, let's go."

Indeed, Will did not appear unwilling. Once Aaron was on his back, he picked up his feet and galloped down the pasture.

"Look at him go!" Joel cried excitedly. "He can run."

"Huh," said Allan. "He's not much more than a pony." He turned and went back to the barn.

Elam and Joel stayed in the pasture. It was fun watching Aaron and Will. Jim seemed to think so too. He ran along beside Will, barking and barking. Every now and then he ran over to Joel and looked up at him as if to ask, "Did you see that? Isn't this fun?"

After a while Aaron rode back to the gate and dismounted. "Your turn now," he said to Elam.

"Okay," said Elam. Joel watched admiringly as he swung onto Will's back. Elam held the little horse back to a slow trot at first, but soon he was cantering too.

Aaron stood beside Joel, watching. "Where's Allan?" he asked after a moment.

Joel shook his head. "I don't know."

"I wish he'd come too. I think he would like to

ride," Aaron said. "Shall we go find him?"

Joel hesitated. Aaron's eyes shone with eagerness. He realized Aaron really wanted his brother to have a good time too. "Okay," he said and followed Aaron to the barn to hunt for Allan.

The barn door was standing open. Aaron opened his mouth to call Allan. Then he stopped. Out of sight from the boys, they heard Dad's voice. "We want you to get along with each other. You know it is wrong to make fun of your brothers."

There was a pause. Joel shivered. Maybe he shouldn't be listening.

Then came Allan's voice, "Sometimes they act as if they don't want to play with me."

Joel was amazed. He had never dreamed Allan might feel this way! Aaron looked surprised too.

Instinctively, Aaron knew what to do. He ran into the barn calling, "Allan! Where are you? Come and take a ride on Will!"

Joel smiled and walked away. Aaron was showing his brother he really did want to play with him! Joel saw Elam coming through the pasture gate with Will. Joel ran over, calling, "I think Allan is coming for a ride too."

"Oh?" said Elam in surprise.

"See? There he comes."

Allan walked out of the barn with his head down and his hands in his pockets. Without a word, he took Will's bridle and mounted the horse.

Elam and Joel and Aaron watched Allan riding away. Each of them was wearing a big smile.

The next afternoon, Mom asked Joel to help her weed the garden while the other boys worked in the barn. Mary was weeding in another corner of the patch. "You go down that side of the carrot row, Joel," Mom instructed, "and I'll take this side. It's easy to pull weeds when the soil is soft after a rain."

"All this rain really makes the weeds grow," Joel observed.

"Yes," Mother replied. They worked awhile in silence. Then she asked, "Did you and the others have a good time riding Will yesterday?"

"Yes. Well, I didn't ride, but Allan did."

"That's good," said Mom.

Joel thought of what he and Aaron had heard in the barn. "Mom, we heard Allan say we don't like to play with him."

"I know," said Mom.

Joel chuckled. "Of course. Dad told you." After a pause he added, "It's funny, isn't it? All the time *we* thought Allan didn't like to play with *us*."

"Do you remember," Mom asked slowly. "I tried to tell you Allan may be having a hard time with all these changes too?"

"I guess I didn't really believe you," Joel confessed. "But I do now."

Mom looked toward the barn. "I see the boys are leading Will to the pasture again. He doesn't seem like the same horse when Aaron is around. Why, Will is actually prancing!"

Joel stopped weeding to watch as Allan mounted Will. "I guess it's a good thing we have that horse."

"We learned a few lessons from him, didn't we?" Mom asked gently. Joel felt his face grow warm. *Yes, he had needed those lessons in willingness.*

Mom went on, "Even though it appears Will has been helping the boys make adjustments, let's not forget who is our best help and our best friend. The Bible says—I think in Proverbs—'There is a friend that sticketh closer than a brother.' Jesus is such a friend to us, closer than a brother. He is always with us, whatever we go through."

Joel nodded. He repeated slowly, "'Closer than a brother.'" Then, smiling, he added, "And closer than a horse called Willing."

Christian Light Publications, Inc., is a nonprofit, conservative Mennonite publishing company providing Christ-centered, Biblical literature including books, Gospel tracts, Sunday school materials, summer Bible school materials, and a full curriculum for Christian day schools and homeschools. Though produced primarily in English, some books, tracts, and school materials are also available in Spanish.

For more information about the ministry of CLP or its publications, or for spiritual help, please contact us at:

Christian Light Publications, Inc.
P. O. Box 1212
Harrisonburg, VA 22803-1212

Telephone—540-434-0768
Fax—540-433-8896
E-mail—info@clp.org
www.clp.org